Where Does Kissing End?

Where Does Kissing End?

Kate Pullinger

Library of Congress Catalog Card Number: 92-60141

British Library Cataloguing in Publication Data

Pullinger, Kate
Where Does Kissing End?
I. Title
813.54 [F]

ISBN 1-85242-277-7

The lyrics from "Behind Closed Doors", on page 88, are reproduced by kind permission of Warner Chappell Music Ltd.

First published 1992
by Serpent's Tail, 4 Blackstock Mews, London N4
and 401 West Broadway #2, New York, NY 10012

Set in 12/15 Bembo by
Countour Typesetters, Southall, London
Printed in Denmark by Nørhaven A/S, Viborg

Where does biting start?
Where does kissing end?

H.J. Stenning

I would like to thank the following people who read early drafts and gave valued advice: Mandy Rose, Mark Ainley and Frances Coady. Rachel Calder was absolutely steadfast and reassuring; Pat Walters remained hopeful at all times. Simon Mellor did all these things and more.

I would also like to thank Hawthornden Castle International Retreat For Writers for a five week stay there in 1990 and the MacDowell Colony for a month in 1992.

". . . May the earth not receive him"; "May the ground not consume him"; "May the earth not digest thee"; "May the black earth spew thee up"; "Mayest thou remain incorrupt"; "May the earth not loose thee" . . .; "May the ground reject thee"; "Mayest thou become in the grave like rigid wood"; "May the ground reject him wholly"; . . .

". . . We have next to mention a still more remarkable perversion of the love-instinct, namely, the wish to die together with the person one loves . . . what one has in death one has for ever . . ."

from "The Vampire", **On The Nightmare**, Ernest Jones (1910)

S

Mina Savage was born the illegitimate child of parents themselves both illegitimate. Her mother, Lucy Savage, had what she called a "husband" who refused to marry her. Harry Summers had started coming into the shop not long after Lucy first began working there. "Meet me for a drink after work," he said one day.

"Me?" replied Lucy looking around.

Lucy found Harry, a man nearly twenty years her senior, extremely attractive. Whenever they met, which even then was no more than once a fortnight, he was attentive. One evening Harry told Lucy he thought she was sexy. "Me?" Lucy replied. No one had ever said anything like that to her before. If Harry thought she was sexy then she really must be sexy and before she knew what was happening they were lovers.

Harry liked to take his pleasures in many places and, although he was not religious, a freak storm in his moral sphere had made him believe that marriage vows were somehow sacred. He would not wed Lucy Savage nor any other woman with whom he had slept for fear of sacrilege. As he spent very little time with women who would not sleep with him he remained stalwartly single.

Lucy assumed that Harry would marry her one day and when he did not she continued to assume it even when she found herself pregnant and still single.

Mina entered the world screaming. The sterilized hospital room reverberated with her cries, drowning out the moans of her mother. She entered the world drenched in blood and foetal fluid – it clogged her nose, her ears, her mouth. Warm water ran red down the drain as the nurse bathed her shocked little body. The baby's glazed, unfocused eyes did not notice who held her and although Lucy knew the raw facts of life – that what she did with Harry was responsible for this child, or rather, what she did not do with Harry with regards to contraception was responsible for this child – she could not quite imagine from where Mina had arrived.

But, she had arrived. The bastard child had her eyes open on the world at last. She could taste it even then, newly born, fists flailing.

Mina and Stephen are in bed. Mina is on top of Stephen. His eyes are closed, his hands grip her breasts. He wishes she would push harder onto him. She wants this to go on and on. She only feels really happy when she is giving someone pleasure. She only feels whole when torn apart. No other sensation – no other emotion – can be trusted.

Mina pushes down on Stephen's cock, her cunt liquid, her eyes rolling back into her head. She moans and grinds her pelvis – he thinks she might break his back. Before she stops he finds himself beginning to come. He tries to hold on but can not. Mina feels she can do anything. There is nothing else like this. Stephen feels faint, his face turned into the pillow; he will let Mina do anything to him.

Harry Summers would not allow Lucy Savage to give

her daughter his name and only once, in a moment of sentimentality as he gazed at the newborn's black eyes which were, he knew, a reflection of his own, did he admit to having any part in the proceedings. "It's enough to make you understand what sex is for," he said. Harry regretted this transgression later though, and generally referred to Mina as "that Savage bitch" or "Lucy's bastard-girl".

The fact that Harry was also a bastard did nothing to soften his attitude. His own mother, Hilda Summers, claimed that his father had been either a sailor, a soldier, or a travelling salesman, depending upon her mood. Hilda had a "reputation" in the community in which she lived. She had turned down an offer of marriage from an ageing bank manager when she was nineteen and no one had ever forgiven her. Hilda enjoyed being single and was only too happy to indulge in self-satisfied smugness when listening to her married friends' tales of woe. She did not take lovers as a matter of course but limited herself to rare encounters similar to the one during which she conceived Harry. That Harry himself would later refuse to marry made perfect sense to her.

Hilda carried the burden of her child's illegitimacy throughout her life without pausing for embarrassment or even too much thought. Everyone else knew the identity of Harry's father. George Varney, the local married butcher, had let lust slice through him over a slab of beef one balmy afternoon. He was an Italian who had changed his real name, Giovanni Varni, when he immigrated as a young man. Hilda was a regular customer and she and George frequently shared a flirtatious joke. She was smiling as she walked into the shop that day. A few people took note when the butcher put his "Back in 10 minutes" sign in the window. When he and the woman who had tempted him got off that flayed side of a cow, Hilda Summers was pregnant as well as covered in blood but neither of them ever admitted to the connection.

Hilda never told Harry who his father was but, like Mina, Harry knew. Varney's name was whispered to him in the classroom by boys Harry would then beat up after school. "The butcher is not your father," he would make the boy repeat. "You don't have any father at all."

Mina's maternal grandmother, Elsa Savage, was dead. Elsa had always claimed that Lucy had no father, that she was the child of a "night visitation". Whether she meant an intruder or some kind of dark spirit was never clear – whenever Lucy asked, as she did occasionally, Elsa would shiver and give a version of either "Was not a man like I've ever seen before" or "Like the Baby Jesus, Lucy, you came to me without my having carnal awareness of any man or boy." Lucy had to content herself with being the child of a frail, superstitious woman who died when her daughter was sixteen, leaving her to be the child of no one.

Ever hopeful of making him promise something, Lucy Savage took Harry Summers into her flat several evenings a month for well over twenty years. It was always the same. Harry would arrive and Lucy would get rid of Mina by locking her into her bedroom or, when the child was older, sending her out to play. Lucy would then bolt the door of the flat and attempt to make Harry Summers a happy man. Harry was large and growing larger with age and he liked to sit in Lucy's big chair and have her force herself down onto him. He also liked Lucy to be naked while he remained almost fully clothed. This was how Mina had been conceived and this is what Mina saw as she peered through the letterbox one rainy afternoon when she had not found anyone to play with in the street.

On the day she was born Lucy and Mina were strangers and this was how they remained. They did not grow to know each other; it was as though neither could figure out who the other was. They loved each other, as family members must, but Lucy felt there was something inexplicable about her child. She was always vaguely surprised to find the little girl there and, although she was kind to her, there was something missing. "Oh, it's you," she would say in the mornings as though startled to find someone else in the flat. In return Mina ignored her mother, not interested in her beyond the demands of infancy, not concerned with what Lucy did or thought. Lucy felt Mina behaved as though she did not really need a mother; from the beginning there was a barrier between them.

But Mina was interested in Harry. She would perform for him when he came around and hated her mother for shooing her away; she would fight for Harry's kisses. Whenever he scooped her up and said "Hello my little blossom" Mina would glance at her mother while Lucy tried hard not to wonder why Harry never called her names like that. Lucy worked hard in life, Harry was her only weakness, so it was not through her that Mina learned the fine art of flirtation. But somewhere, somehow, the girl did acquire the skills of a charmer and Harry was the first man on whom she could practise.

Harry, of course, was a fool for it. The little girl batted her great black eyes at him and he batted his own back. She snuggled in his lap with her arm around his neck, attempting to engage him in complicated conversations about sweetshops and new clothes. After dinner he would hoist Mina onto his knee and they would tickle each other while Lucy did the washing-up. Only when Lucy grew impatient with the desire to have Harry to herself would Mina be sent off to play. And then Lucy would have an easy time regaining his attention while Harry flattered himself with the thought of having produced such a child. His pride gave Lucy much pleasure. Mina would always return to find her mother happy and calm, airing out the room and clearing up after Harry's visit.

Harry enjoyed watching Mina grow, pronouncing at regular intervals on how beautiful she would be. "You'll break hearts," he would whisper into Mina's sweet-smelling ear, "just like me."

"Mina," Lucy complained to Harry one evening, "has taken to biting. Especially after you've been here. Whenever she wants something which I won't allow she gets so cross she bites me. I slap her then she bites even harder. The other day she made me bleed."

Harry laughed. Parental advice was not his forte. He blamed Lucy for everything Mina did wrong. "You're too strict," he replied, and then later, "You're not strict enough," was all he would say.

When Mina was a pretty three year old – swift smiles and frilly dresses – Harry took her to visit his mother, an honour Lucy had never been given. Hilda still lived where Harry had grown up. She still used the same butcher.

Mina hid behind Harry's leg when she saw the door open. The old woman laughed and bent down, taking Mina by the arm. "Come here," she said sternly, "I want to look at you." She studied Mina's face, then looked at Harry and back down at the child again. "Yes," she said nodding, unwilling to say more. Mina was wide-eyed with fear.

Hilda took her son and his daughter into her kitchen. She handed Mina, now sitting on Harry's broad lap, a biscuit. "It's a good thing to be a bastard," she said suddenly. "Not having a father gives a person a certain freedom. You haven't got all that Daddy is God business to get over. One less adult to be disappointed by. One less person to have to compete with. Not that girls compete with their fathers so much as flirt with them. But, anyway, fatherless children do all right in this world. Right, Harry?" she said, looking from Mina to her son.

Despite the fact that when he came around Harry would slip Lucy a bit of cash, life was not easy. Lucy worked and Mina came home from school to an empty flat, but this was never much of a problem for either of them. Mina liked things best when she had them to herself, even when she was small.

By the time Mina had been at school a couple of years her mother was made assistant floor manager at the shop. Lucy had no interests outside her job, her daughter and Harry – on the rare occasions when she went out it was with people from work. She was too busy to notice the passage of time, at the shop during the day and then at home with Mina in the evening. A decade floated by unnoticed like a cloud in the night sky.

Mina thinks of herself and Lucy as "broken". She never uses the word "family" to describe the unit which she and her mother make.

One afternoon when Mina is twelve she is at a neighbour's watching over their four year old. The little girl has fallen asleep on the floor in front of the television. Mina is bored; she wanders into the Ogilvy's bedroom and begins to open cupboards and drawers. Myra Ogilvy wears her hair in a small but stiff blonde beehive which Mina admires; she also wears an enormous amount of make-up. Mina tries on all the shades of eyeshadow and lipstick. She opens the closet and touches Myra Ogilvy's clothes – there are rows of shiny rayon, sequins and lace. After a while Mina gets bored with this as well; she lies down on the floor.

Mina has one cheek buried in the Ogilvy's carpet when she notices a pile of magazines under the bed. She drags them out, brushing away the dust. Some have torn plastic wrappers still clinging to them. They have names which even a twelve year old finds vaguely comical. Mina opens two at a time and begins to look at the pictures and read what text there is. Soon she is surrounded by naked bodies.

Mina knows about sex, she has heard a lot about it at school and she has done a fair amount of experimenting with boys from around the neighbourhood. She knows she can get things by flirting, by being sure of herself. But she has never seen pictures. Photographs have a certain reality; they have what look like real people in them. The girl is spellbound by the magazines, suddenly noticing how hard the floor feels beneath her body. As she turns the pages she begins to rock against the carpet. She is getting very warm when she hears the front door open.

As quickly as she can she shoves the magazines back under the bed. She goes into the bathroom and washes off the make-up and then walks into the sitting-room. The Ogilvys are talking to their daughter. They do not notice the colour of Mina's face. She asks them if they would like her to babysit the next weekend. To her great excitement they say yes.

Mina learns all about a certain kind of sex at the

Ogilvy's. She knows that the sex in the pictures is not "ordinary". She knows this is not what Lucy and Harry do together – she has seen them often enough. Mina has never told anyone about the moments she snatches away from her mother through the letterbox – brief moments when there is no one on the landing of the block of flats to wonder what she is doing. And she tells no one about the magazines either.

Mina makes herself come for the first time on the floor of Myra Ogilvy's bedroom, lipstick smeared all around her mouth. She keeps pushing herself against the carpet, leaving the magazine open at a picture she finds particularly surprising. Before she knows what is happening she feels herself lifted up into orgasm: it makes her hot, it makes her weak, it makes her happy. She turns the page and does it again, turns the page and does it again. And then she stops only because she can hear the Ogilvy's little girl calling from where she sits in front of the TV.

That night in bed Mina touches herself between her legs. She is sore where her pubic bone has rubbed against the floor but she feels pleased for having made this discovery. It is a physical pleasure more intense than any other she has felt. This is something for her alone; this is something she can control. That fiery moment is hers. Mina is sure life will be more interesting from now on.

Later that night, Mina's sleep is disturbed by nightmares. She dreams of Harry standing at the end of her bed, naked, his penis painfully large. He threatens to hold her down and prise her legs open. "Your mother lets me do it," is all he says. "Your mother never objects."

Harry slept on his back, always had and always would. Hilda had tried to cure him of this when he was a child – from the age of two his snoring had disturbed her sleep. Harry snored like the end of the world, like an earthquake, a volcano, a nuclear melt-down. Hilda was the first to suffer; since then he had kept women awake all over London.

After visiting Lucy and Mina, Harry would always snore very loudly, as if exceptionally sure of his place in the world. On this night he had left the window open and his snores could be heard in the street. At two a.m. his room filled with a soft light as though near dawn. It swirled over his bed in the eddies between his raucous sighs, settling down over his body. Harry spluttered in his sleep and moved his hands away from himself, to his sides, as though pinned down or flattened by a kind of weight. His breath became rapid, his snoring subsided almost completely. He woke when he came, gasping and jerking, the sheets speckled with blood and cum. His room went dark again.

Mina spent a lot of time by herself. She was not very good at making friends and even worse at keeping them. Girls found her intimidating and aloof. She sparked off feelings they did not like having: envy, jealousy, malice. It was not the way Mina looked or talked or simply was that annoyed them but something more basic, animal.

Mina liked being a girl. Girlhood was freedom to her; she loved jewellery and clothes, lipstick and skin cream. When she was very young the only women she ever really remembered were those who were perfumed and made-up. This was not something she had learned from Lucy – her mother's dress sense was utilitarian, she could not afford frills. Whenever she went out in the evening Mina would beg Lucy to paint her lips, wear earrings, a smarter dress. Lucy usually went along with Mina's requests just to keep her quiet, but she was puzzled by her daughter's intensity. Sometimes it seemed to Lucy that the only thing Mina really cared about was her own appearance. She was obsessive and insistent about what she wore and how she wore it. She seemed to take glossy women's magazines literally.

Mina was often criticized for this dedication to what other girls thought of as pandering to the boys. But Mina didn't care; she knew the boys liked it. And those same young women could not help but admire her when, in high heels, Mina negotiated the steepest staircase or the roughest pavement, her lipsticked mouth taunting the catcallers just as caustically as anyone else.

Mina had that pale look that is always fashionable. She had an ability to make a boy feel he was the most interesting person in the room. When she rested her eyes upon someone, when she gave him her full attention, that boy would feel as though he had never been listened to before. Young men asked her to go to the cinema, they wanted her to go to parties, to dance with them. To a certain kind of boy Mina would say yes: yes to the handsome ones, to the ones who didn't ask too many questions, to the ones she saw wanted her the most. No to the clumsy ones, to the ones who told jokes, to the ones who talked too much about themselves.

Mina was not interested in school activities, or gossip. In the classroom she spent a lot of time staring into space and would have been called a dreamer had her wits not been so sharp.

One day at school as the bell rang and all the other students got up to go, Mina suddenly slumped forward onto her desk. The teacher, a young man, rushed over as she began to sit up again. She looked at him blankly as he repeated her name and then, once her head had cleared, she refused to be escorted to the infirmary.

That night Mina's body was racked with violent menstrual cramps. After taking several of her mother's pain-killers she lay rubbing her abdomen, waiting for the pain to subside.

When Mina had first begun to menstruate she often had to spend sleepless nights doing leg-lifts and sit-ups to try to massage her convulsing muscles. She usually bled very heavily for several days and this was when it was most common for her to suffer blackouts. At night, she'd be standing by the window and then, later, would find herself flat out on the bed. Sometimes she would wake up in another room of the flat, even her mother's bedroom, and would have to sneak away. Other nights she would wake standing beside her open window, the dirty smell of London filling the room.

Usually Mina was able to cope with bad nights and still be calm and wide-awake during the day. But the day after she fainted in the classroom she passed out again after school. She was sitting with her current flame (Mina's flames burned brightly, however brief) in a bus shelter – they were kissing. His lips were very soft. He had his hand between her legs, his fingers touching the creases in her jeans.

Everything goes dark and bright at the same time. She feels powerful and wild although disabled, unable to actually do anything. It is as if there is something greater, something stronger, dwelling deep inside her. It overwhelms her; she loses herself. This is not an entirely unpleasant feeling; Mina has felt this way before.

Suddenly Mina felt the boy shaking her. She was leaning heavily on him, her lips grazing his neck, the top of her head banging against the glass of the shelter. "Are you all right?" he repeated. "Are you okay?"

Mina sat up and breathed deeply. It was as though something had passed through her and was gone again. She told the boy she was fine, she smiled and said that his kisses had been too much for her. As she went to lay her head on his shoulder she noticed there was a little blood on the inside of his collar and a matching spot on his neck. An old song from the fifties that she had heard on the radio, "Lipstick on Your Collar", came to her mind and she started to giggle.

The boy was trying to get his hand inside the back of her shirt again. "What are you laughing at?" he asked. Mina shook her head. "Come on, tell me," he said. "What is it?" Mina licked his bottom lip and then kissed him to stop any further questions.

That night Mina lies awake chastising herself. She knows it is important to remain in control, to stop fainting, to stop her body collapsing in public. She does not think there is a problem, nor does she think about what causes it, what it means. She does not want to be watched, she does not want to be noticed in this way. She must practise being strong, must make herself impenetrable. There are ways, lots of ways, for her to gain strength.

*

The first time Mina ever had intercourse was with a boy she met at a party on the other side of London. Despite the sexual activity of her friends she had managed to put it off with her claim, a truthful one, that the boys she knew bored her. The boy she met at this party looked older and was a good dancer. He did not have a lot to say. Mina asked if he wanted to go outside. It was drizzling as they stood under the eave of the garden shed, one shoulder dry, the other wet. They kissed and Mina pretended she knew what she was doing – she had thought about it enough to be convincing. She undid his trousers, he pulled down her knickers and they fucked standing up, his back and her arms around him getting wetter and wetter. Mina did not feel pain, although as he came, which he did very quickly, she caught her nail on his cheek just in front of his ear. As the blood began to come to the surface of his skin she kissed it away. His knees buckled and he moaned as his penis slid out of her. Then he held her and she kissed him over and over, her hand sticky between her legs as she made herself come.

*

Harry's mother Hilda died in the hospital where Mina was born. She died of old age, ailing suddenly and completely. To Hilda aging meant a general falling apart which she did not like; as her hearing got worse she prepared herself to die.

Hilda had warned Harry years before that when she was ready she would simply go. "There are worse things than living a long life and dying happily," she said. "And when I'm gone you will be all alone in the world, Harry. There is nothing wrong with being alone in the world. I have you and you, well, I suppose you have got the girl Mina," – Harry moved to interrupt, he had never said, not even to Hilda, that he thought Mina was his child – "although she does not really belong to you, I know. I'd watch out for her though," she said stopping Harry from speaking yet again. "There is something worrying about her, I'm sure." Harry shook his head but as far as Hilda was concerned the subject was closed and she began to complain about the Government.

When Hilda became ill Harry felt angry with her; when she entered the hospital he was enraged by the doctors and nurses whom he accused of not helping her.

Hilda was soon past telling him to calm down and shut up and he would not listen to anyone else. Late one evening breathing became difficult and Hilda died in her sleep. As Harry watched his mother's life drain from her body a huge fury filled him. He terrorized the nursing staff on night duty and reproached them for treating his mother like an unimportant old woman; he threatened to take Hilda's body away from the hospital. He threw a bedpan belonging to another patient on the ward against the wall. Several of the elderly ladies applauded. When Mina suddenly appeared he took hold of her shoulders and shook her, shouting "What are you doing here?"

Mina did not know why she had decided to come to the hospital so late that night. She knew Hilda was there although she had not been to visit the old woman for years. Unable to sleep she got dressed and took a bus to the hospital.

Harry stopped shaking Mina and began to cry. Behind him Hilda lay still on the bed. Mina knew without going any nearer that she was dead. Harry stood with his face buried in his hands. Mina had never seen a man cry before except on television; it made her feel big and him seem small. She did not attempt to touch Harry or to speak. She just stood there and stared. Several feet away a harassed nurse watched them both.

Mina looked at Hilda again. She wondered how it felt to die. Hilda looked composed, as if she had simply left her body without violence, without attempting to linger. Mina wondered at what point she had ceased to be human.

Harry stopped crying abruptly and straightened his back. "Don't look at her," he hissed. "she's gone."

Over the next few days Harry spent all his time making arrangements for Hilda's funeral. He had her body laid out for viewing in a room full of flowers at the funeral parlour and hired a limousine for the trip to the cemetery. For the roof of the hearse he ordered a wreath of orange tiger lilies, Hilda's favourite, spelling "Mother". He went to a fitting for a morning suit and gave both Mina and Lucy money to buy new dresses, "the blackest black you can find," he specified. Lucy wondered if Harry would let her stand next to him in the cemetery. With shame, she found herself looking forward to the event. Mina was happiest about the new dress; Lucy had never allowed her to wear black before. It was a colour to which she aspired.

Harry had arranged with the owner of the funeral parlour, a business acquaintance, to be allowed to spend his nights watching over his mother. For three nights after her death he sat beside her and gazed at her face, grey beneath the beige make-up. Then on the fourth night, the night before the funeral, Harry succumbed to sleep. He had been at Lucy's to survey the new dresses. Lucy cooked him dinner and even Mina was solicitous toward him. They both urged him to go home and spend a night in his own bed in order to prepare for the next day.

Hilda's body disappeared that night. At the funeral

parlour there was no sign of breaking and entering, nor even breaking and exiting. The coffin was empty, the flowers only slightly disturbed.

Harry's wrath was incomparable. He virtually destroyed the room where Hilda had been and he very nearly beat up the undertaker who saved himself by displaying an outrage almost as great as Harry's. Both men calmed down over a bottle of brandy which was kept handy for overwrought mourners. Once drunk, Harry began to find the situation funny. It was just like his mother to confound all expectations.

Lucy, arriving at the funeral parlour with Mina an hour before the ceremony was due to begin, was appalled by what she saw. Harry was lying in the coffin with a rose in his mouth while the undertaker pronounced solemn vows over him. Mina began to laugh.

"Have you called the police?" asked Lucy, her voice shrill.

"What good would that do?" replied Harry, his eyes still closed. "Put up a missing corpse poster – 'Have you seen this woman, 5′9″, grey hair, decaying'?"

"She hasn't just walked out of here," Lucy said, nearly shouting. "For all you know her body could have been stolen by a pervert. I think you should do something about it." Harry, however, was not convinced. As far as he was concerned his mother was dead and that was all that really mattered.

The funeral went ahead with a closed empty coffin. Harry sobered up and everyone behaved with dignity. Mina was pleased by the splendour of the occasion, impressed by the graveyard and the words of the vicar. The other mourners included all of Hilda's aging, now widowed, female friends and the retired butcher George Varney. Harry stood next to the undertaker and nowhere near Lucy who shed a few tears behind her black lace veil. Mina stood leaning into the cutting wind. She decided she felt perfectly at ease with death.

Hilda's missing body was not mentioned again.

Lucy was surprised when, one week after school had finished, Mina came into the shop and said, "I've got a job."

"A job?" said her mother.

"Yes, in that travel agency, you know." Lucy, who had never left the country, nodded. "Aren't you pleased?"

"Yes, well, yes . . ." Lucy mumbled. Mina smiled and then left as abruptly as she had arrived. Lucy stood very still, her face pale, until someone asked her what was wrong. "Mina's got a job, and not just a Saturday one," she said.

A dogsbody job in a travel agency suited Mina for the time being. She made cups of tea for the staff, did the typing and ingratiated herself with the boss. Popular with the customers, she was soon booking coach tours and daytrips to France. Her first pay cheque had been a complete revelation. She suddenly realized what life was all about: work and money meant freedom. At first she spent most of her wages on clothes. She went to lots of parties and stayed out late, arguing with Lucy the next morning. She lied continually about where she had been and what she had done. Her mother did not expect to be confided in but was still as shocked as always by her daughter's wilfulness.

"Just because I don't want to be a martyr and a hermit like you . . ." Mina shouted.

"Men," Lucy said, hesitating before offering advice, "men will take what you let them, Mina, nothing more and nothing less."

One evening, not long after Hilda's funeral, Lucy cooked Harry's favourite dish, the only thing she knew how to make that had garlic in it. Harry had a thing for garlic, he thought it made food taste exotic. She looked forward to feeding him.

But today Harry was late, later than usual. Lucy cleaned the bathroom, tidied her bedroom and then, bored, ventured into Mina's room. Feeling guilty already, she looked in Mina's closet and under her bed, but everything was neat, almost pristine, as though the girl did not really live there. Lucy opened the drawer second to the top in the bureau which she had bought for Mina when she was a baby.

Outside on the landing Harry paused, his breath short, his heart pounding.

In the drawer Lucy saw birth control pills.

Outside, Harry composed himself and then knocked.

Lucy slammed the drawer shut.

The smell of cooking greeted Harry as Lucy opened the door of her flat. "Ah," he said smiling, "you've made my favourite." He walked in stooping slightly.

"You look tired," said Lucy. Harry's face was red and his breath seemed laboured. He frowned, it was the wrong thing for her to have said. "That's a nice shirt," she added quickly.

"And you look well yourself," he replied with forced jocularity. "Where's Minnie Mouse?"

"In Paris."

"Paris?"

"Yes. She can get very cheap deals through work and she was so keen, I couldn't stop her from going by herself. She's so independent, you know what she . . ." Lucy paused, remembering the pills. They seemed too real, threatening, a tangible reminder of her daughter's total separateness. Lucy had no way of knowing what Mina did nor who she was out there in the world. The discovery of the pills made her feel powerless.

"God only knows the kind of people she meets, gallivanting all over the show like she does," Harry said, still grumpy.

"Well, young people do seem to have a lot of money these days," Lucy replied. She could not tell Harry about the pills.

"I've always said Mina was clever enough to make lots of money," (Lucy heard "unlike you"). "Next thing she'll own that travel company."

"Oh, I don't know." Lucy spoke over her shoulder as she backed out of the tiny kitchen. She carried a pot over to the table where Harry had already sat down expectantly. The blood was draining from his face and now he looked very pale. As Lucy served him she noticed he was breathing in short, abrupt gasps. She said nothing and sat down to eat with him.

After dinner, Harry went over to his chair. He was thinking about Mina and how long it had been since she had sat on his knee. Harry missed Mina's easy-going familiarity. It had taken several years to notice that she had become all breasts and elbows but when he did it came as a shock. Harry did not always make love to Lucy when he came around these days but it was seeing the girl that he really missed. Lucy could sense this and she tried to compensate by being more attentive, even tarting herself up a bit. But Harry was not all that interested. Some evenings he would sit in the chair and look at the door as if he expected Mina to walk through at any moment. But, of course, she didn't, she was always somewhere else these days.

Lucy finished clearing up and then walked back into the sitting room where Harry was sitting in silence. He looked as though he might have fallen asleep. "Are you feeling all right?" she asked.

Harry jumped, said yes, and then seemed to rally around. "Come here," he said to Lucy, "take your knickers off." Lucy blushed and smiled and did as she was told. She stood in front of the chair and Harry fingered her absent-mindedly. She squirmed to stop him from hurting her. Harry looked up at her face as if suddenly remembering where he was. He stood, undoing his trousers. Lifting Lucy's skirt, he put his hand behind her right knee and pulled up her leg. He pushed into her awkwardly, his large belly in the way.

"Do you still want me Harry?" whispered Lucy. His reply was muffled, his face buried in her hair. Close to tears, Lucy moved her hips slowly. She wished Harry desired her all the time.

As abruptly as he had stood, Harry sat down again. The rough movement of his lungs was audible. He had lost his erection and when he opened his eyes he looked plaintive and afraid. Then his eyes closed and he fell forward. Lucy cried out, grabbed his shoulders and, when she couldn't move him, ran to the telephone.

While Harry struggled in Lucy's flat, Mina was fucking a stranger in a foreign city.

Fucking around was something Mina did mercilessly; it was something at which she was skilled. In the early days she had done it by exhibiting a raw hunger so pure that no one could resist. "She wants it. She really wants it," was all a boy could think. With a bit of age and practice her technique had become more refined; now the man always thought it was him doing the conquering. Most men could not even remember what happened, she took that much away with her. All they were left with was a vague memory of her smell; she was not in the habit of exchanging telephone numbers and names.

Mina wanted to begin to travel as soon as she was able. She had scarcely been out of London before, but planes, trains and ships seemed natural to her. It was the anonymity that appealed to her, the idea that no one would know what she was doing, who she was. She would be able to change her clothes, her hair, her way of speaking, several times a day. She packed a little suitcase as though she had done it hundreds of times, knowing just what to take.

For this first trip she decided to travel to Paris. The grey city seemed small to her, dense with familiar landmarks. She tried to avoid the places with queues, the places full of foreigners like herself. She walked down Rue Faubourg St Denis, in and out of shops, through the markets; she paused to sit in cafés and eat toasted sandwiches; she watched people. The little hotel room she booked through her agency had a view of a well between high walls. In the evening she would go to the cinema and then find somewhere to eat.

Bored in the Louvre one afternoon, Mina followed a young French student who carried a sketchpad under one arm. He soon noticed her and they spoke to each other – bad French, bad English. They went to sit outside in the weak winter sun on steps leading down to the Seine.

The boy wanted to be a painter but was studying graphic art because someone had told him it was more practical. Already he was frustrated and a little unhappy – he communicated this to Mina through one-word speeches and elaborate gestures. Mina didn't really care what he wanted to do, the way he looked and spoke was enough. He wore a bulky old jumper and very tight jeans which wrapped around his hips handsomely. When Mina put her hand on his thigh he cheerfully gave up his struggle with conversation. They kissed, touching each other through their clothes. On the walk to Mina's hotel they stopped frequently to admire each other and kiss again. Once they had snuck past the porter and were behind a closed door, the young man was willing and eager.

He wants to be hers. He wants her to take him. He opens himself up, bares himself. He won't mind if she hurts him. It is easy.

Mina arrived back from her weekend in Paris and went straight to work. Lucy rang; the words "Harry is ill" sounded odd, as if familiar. After work, Mina took a bus to the hospital just like the night she went to see Hilda. She wondered if Harry was going to die.

The ward was somewhere in the labyrinth of the sixth floor and when she found him Harry was lying very still in his bed, his eyes closed. Mina looked out the window; straight across the river was Big Ben, hands on seven o'clock, its chimes inaudible through the glass.

When she turned around Harry had opened his eyes. He was not looking at her but somewhere past her, at a point in the sky, "Harry?" said Mina a bit too loudly. "Hello," she continued, blushing. Still Harry did not look at her. Mina found this terrifying. The air in the ward was heavy with the smell of chemicals and something barely hidden, much worse.

"Harry?" Mina spoke again. The other old men began to stare at her openly. She walked closer to the head of the bed. Then she bent over trying to will him to look at her. Slowly, Harry moved his eyes, only his eyes, until they rested on Mina's face. He stared blankly at her chin. She thought he looked very sad but all the old men could see it was Mina who was sad. She could not stop the tears from burning her eyes. Underneath the white blanket Harry looked thin and small. Mina continued to stare at him long after he closed his eyes again. Then she took a bus home.

The next day Mina found a flat of her own. The day after that she moved in.

When Harry went home after one month in the hospital he required a full-time nurse but one was not provided by the state and, despite his hard work, he had little in the way of savings. Harry's speech was slurred as though he was drunk, he stood and walked with great difficulty and seemed to have lost much of his short term memory. However he could see and understand most of what went on around him. For instance, he registered the fact that Mina was disgusted by him.

Mina blamed Harry for his illness. She wanted him to be big and boisterous and when he was not, she felt let down. She did not want him to slobber slightly when he took a drink; she expected him to flirt with her when she brought him things. As Lucy took on the responsibility of caring for her lover, Mina came to visit less and less. She was angry with Harry and thought it fair to express that.

Lucy was not pleased to have Harry at her mercy, dependent on her. She was afraid that, among other things, he would never slide his hand under her skirt again. She was afraid that his being old meant she was old as well.

Harry sat in his chair in his flat and felt the world go on without him. Frustrated by his own disabilities, he kept the television on to dispel his thoughts. He found himself dwelling on the past.

One night, after Lucy had done the washing-up and gone home, Harry saw Hilda. He was sitting in the dark having asked Lucy to turn off the television before she left. He closed his eyes and dozed in the chair. When he opened them again, Hilda was standing before him. She still had on the undertaker's make-up and the white dress which Harry had asked for her to be laid out wearing. When she spoke her voice sounded as though it was travelling through several feet of water.

"I don't like this dress, I look like a bride in it, I'm dead Harry, not getting married." She paused and adjusted a sleeve. "Although I must say I believe the two experiences are similar. You, my son, are slouching. Sit up. Listen Harry, you aren't paying enough attention to that girl." He knew she meant Mina. "I expected that you would watch out for her more. We dead can see things, you know." Harry opened his mouth to interrupt but she prevented him. "Why did you have to go and get sick? Sit up and close your mouth. I liked the flowers on the hearse, that was a nice touch."

Mina has an ugly relationship with herself. This is something she has learned from her mother. However, unlike Lucy who lacks real ambition, Mina is driven without knowing why or by what. Since she was a child she has felt marked out at different times, in different ways. The dizzy spells, the blackouts, her periods of disorientation: there is something Mina has long given up trying to explain. She smothers her own questions with sex and desire, she tries to keep them at bay.

Mina has a recurrent nightmare where she finds herself in a desert, her throat parched. She lies on the ground and listens for the sound of running water. A man appears walking toward her and Mina is deafened by the pounding liquid that courses through his body, the fluids that move, sloshing and pumping, beneath his skin.

When she wakes it takes her a full minute to remember where she is.

Mina does not eat enough because she worries about getting fat. She dyes her dark hair darker because she hates its natural colour; she spends too much money on cosmetics because she dislikes her skin. Her relationship with her own body can only be described as penitential; she strip-searches herself in front of the mirror. Even though she is still very young she fears aging, she fears losing what she has got. But worst of all she does not know that this is what it is to be a woman, she does not realize that all women can feel these things. But Mina does not think in terms of "being a woman": she does not feel part of any sisterhood. Something other makes Mina stand apart; something other makes Mina unspeakably alone.

On her second trip abroad Mina travelled to Amsterdam, a city of left-over hippies and punks, lace curtains and heroin. Mina avoided all of the above; she stayed in a hotel overlooking one of the canals and went for long walks in the late afternoon sun. She found the red-light district by accident and felt both compelled and dismayed by the women in the windows, the curtains pulled back as though on stage.

At night Mina went to dark and low-key bars where people smoked dope and drank beer – Mina herself did not smoke, she disliked the way it made people stupid and sleepy, the way, once stoned, people thought anything was funny. Still Mina hung out in the bars and was sociable. She was waiting for something but she did not pause to think what or whom.

Every night for three nights Mina invited a different man into her hotel room. After letting them buy her drinks all evening she felt she deserved something in return. She took them standing next to the narrow single bed, on the floor, against the cheap wood of the wardrobe. They cried out from the edge of insensibility; she watched them twist and turn. Every morning these men would leave before breakfast, their faces drawn and tired in the white light. When she checked out the receptionist insisted she pay the price of a double room.

Mina went back to London and Lucy who was now exhausted by the strain of working full-time as well as taking care of Harry. Lucy spent part of every evening around at Harry's flat, cooking and cleaning for him. She realized that her new role in Harry's life was wifely but that did not make her feel any happier. It certainly did not seem to be making Harry happy either. He refused to give Lucy her own key. But on the few occasions when she did not visit her arrival the next day was almost too upsetting; Harry had done nothing, not eaten, not shaved, not even turned on the television, things Lucy was becoming increasingly convinced he could do for himself. In her more tired moments she felt as though she had been enslaved.

She asked Mina for help.

"No," her daughter replied.

"Why not? He has been so good to you in the past. You know how much he likes to see you."

"No. I don't want to see him."

"Everybody gets old, Mina. Everybody needs taking care of some day."

"Harry is not old."

"I'm not old either, but I feel it. Just come with me tonight." Lucy was not used to asking for favours. Mina shook her head violently, back and forth, like an angry child. Later, she rang her mother from work and said she would go to see Harry but only if Lucy did not come. Lucy agreed, put the phone down and felt relieved. She went back to the re-order form which she needed to complete.

Mina took a bus over to Harry's flat, climbing the stairs which smelt of piss. When she knocked on the door there was no reply. She knocked more loudly and heard a muffled voice from somewhere inside. Mina bent over and peered through the letterbox. She could hear Harry shuffling around.

"Harry?" she called out, "It's me, Mina. Let me in." She stood up wishing she had not come. Eventually he got to the door, opening it slowly as if he felt apprehensive about who might be there. "I'm not a fucking Jehovah's Witness you know," Mina said, forcing a laugh.

Harry looked just the same as always, maybe even a little better for having lost some weight. He did not look sick. Without saying a word he turned around and began to walk towards the sitting room in the same laborious shuffle with which he had come to the door. Mina followed behind him, leaning against the wall. The flat smelt stuffy, overwarm.

"Could I have a cup of tea?" Harry asked, once he had sat down. Mina was shocked, she was accustomed to Harry making demands of Lucy but not of her. She went into the kitchen and put the kettle on. Everything was very neat, just the way her mother liked it. She went back into the other room. "Did you bring any biscuits?" he asked.

"Harry, you haven't seen me for months and that's all you've got to say? I'm not Lucy, you know. I haven't come to be your nurse."

Harry looked tired. He peered at Mina as though through a fog. "Come here then," he said suddenly. "Sit on my knee." Mina went automatically. She began to rub his neck like she used to do when she was small. "I get these aches," he said, "in my head. As though there is something in there trying to make itself felt, some kind of knowledge that I've absorbed but not understood, something that would make everything much clearer." He paused. "You never come to visit me."

Mina felt guilty. She shifted her weight on his leg.

"You have got to make sure that you don't do anything wrong. You've got to be careful. Don't mess up. Is it a good job you've got?" Mina nodded. "Well, make a lot of money." The kettle was boiling so Mina got up leaving Harry looking a bit flatter and smaller.

Mina stood in the kitchen moving around the tea things. After finding some biscuits she put them on the tray which she carried into the sitting room. Harry seemed to have fallen asleep. Mina could not bear to look at him. She wanted to talk to him like before. She wanted him to give her bits of practical advice which she could then ignore, not vague words that sounded more like warnings.

She decided to leave. She put her coat on quietly in the next room but as she went towards the door Harry shouted "Mina," and then again "Mina," with great force. She walked to the door of the sitting room. Her mother's lover was standing upright. "We never had a father, did we?" he said. "Give us a kiss."

Hesitating, Mina stepped backwards and then forward. She rushed at Harry, almost tripping before stopping in front of him. He held her shoulders and then kissed her abruptly. When she turned away he patted her on the bum and as she left they both felt a bit better than before.

*

Stephen felt faint when he first sighted Mina. It was as if he recognized her, although he was sure they had never met. He had gone into a travel agency to book a flight to New York. This time he was going without his parents.

Mina was sitting at her desk. On the wall behind her was a poster from Jamaica. Stephen looked at her and then looked at the picture and only just managed to stop himself from saying something gauche about wanting to lie on a beach with her. He cleared his throat and Mina looked at him. Her eyes had been focused on the door; she was waiting for an important client to come in.

"May I help you?" she asked and Stephen thought he might die from pleasure at the sound of her voice.

"Yes," he replied, "as a matter of fact, you can. I want to fly to New York."

"When would you like to fly?"

"In about a fortnight."

"Just let me see what we've got that might be suitable," Mina replied, turning to her computer and picking up a pen. Stephen searched his brain for something entertaining to say, something devastatingly witty and urbane. After a few minutes during which he stared at the top of her head Mina gave him the details. Then she made a phone call, consulting him over dates and times. He signed the forms without asking the price which Mina then volunteered. "Do you want me to post the ticket to you?"

"No," he said, "I'll come and pick it up." Mina explained that it would be ready the next week. Then she looked at Stephen expectantly, while he sat and stared at her. After a few long moments he stood, banging his knee.

Stephen Smith carried his family history inside himself like a stone he had swallowed and never passed. The story of his parents' early lives was absolutely indigestible but part of him nonetheless. Born in London long years after his parents had fled their own country, educated in English schools, in English ways, in English, Stephen always felt that beneath his near-perfect skin-tight Englishness lived another different self; it was like a new winter coat that fits perfectly.

For Stephen being Jewish in London was a coded, mysterious thing. The relatives he knew who had emigrated to North America lived with their Jewishness more openly; they enjoyed a kind of popular symbolic Jewishness that involved the eating of gefilte fish, the financial support of tree-planting in Israel and a mass celebration of festivals and religious holidays. They gave each other Channukah cards; they told Jewish jokes. The synagogue and the weddings, circumcisions and funerals that took place inside it served as a social focus in New York and Montréal for his parents' generation; children were less religious but good-naturedly so.

But Stephen grew up in a part of London with no Jewish presence and he lacked this sense of place and belonging that other Jews from more closely-knit communities seemed to cherish. His parents kept some of the traditions but they were anxious for Stephen and his brother, Joseph, to be as English as possible, not marked by difference in any way. Ben and Anna did not see any point in insisting upon the very things for which they had been forced to leave Romania. Apart from his family Stephen did not know many other Jews, certainly none who participated in the traditions. In fact he had felt shock one day during Passover when he had seen groups of yarmulke-wearing little boys on a street in North London.

Stephen's parents had left Eastern Europe with little regret, feeling lucky to have got out when they did. Romania was not "home" like it was for other exiles, growing old while waxing virulent and anti-communist in the bars of Toronto and other cities. Like immigrants the world over, the Smiths had acquired their name in a neat side-step of history, shedding Szekely like an old skin. What Ben and Anna really wanted out of life now was Oxford-educated, independent, successful Londoners for sons and this, for the most part, was what they had got. Stephen and his brother Joseph were assimilated Jews, not tied to the old world but able to live in and full of the new. They did not think those dark mountains which stretch into Hungary were, in any way, part of their souls.

One night when Stephen was still a boy, only fourteen,

he had an extraordinary dream. He had been having this particular kind of dream for some time and he and his mother, who was the one who had to wash the sheets, had stopped being embarrassed about it. Usually Stephen dreamt about female singers or movie stars; a couple of times he was mortified by having dreamt about friends of his mother's and once he actually had a wet dream about Emily Brontë whose book *Wuthering Heights* he had been reading.

But on this windy, November night Stephen went to bed rather late having stayed up to watch a horror film on television. He said goodnight to his mum and dad and went upstairs, past the room where his brother Joseph was already sleeping. He put on his pyjamas, which were too small, banging his knee on the desk. Then he climbed into bed and fell asleep without pausing to think about anything.

Much later Stephen awoke. His blankets had slid onto the floor and he was lying on the bed naked. He felt as though there was something in the room, something hovering overhead. He looked up and in the darkness could see a swirling of colour, a kind of breezy, electric whirlpool, like interference on a television screen. Feeling only vaguely uneasy he lay still, on his back. The moving air, the flecks of colour, settled down over him. There was a strange smell, slightly muddy, almost perfumed.

Stephen felt the bed move, as though someone had sat down on it. He thought of his mother who used to read to him. The bed moved again and he felt a warmth, like a body stretched beside him. Now on top of him. He could not move his arms but he did not really try, he was not frightened. He felt something, a kind of piercing feeling, along his skin, but then that tiny pain was overwhelmed by a surging of desire. He came all over himself and as he came the air around him dissipated and he was left wide awake, all alone. "I came without touching myself," he thought, impressed.

For Stephen the week between buying the ticket and picking it up passed slowly. When it was finally time to go back to the travel agency he found Mina the same as before; polite, efficient and incredibly sexy. "What's your name?" he asked as she checked the spelling of his. Once she had told him it proved difficult to think of anything else to say. He left the office, ticket in hand, demoralized and randy.

At home Stephen slammed plates around the kitchen where Anna sat reading a book on psychoanalysis. "What's wrong sweetheart?" she asked absent-mindedly.

"Nothing!" he shouted.

"That's good," she replied, looking back down at her book. Stephen continued unloading the dishwasher noisily.

Once her boys had become teenagers and her out-dated skills were no longer needed at Ben's office, Anna had begun to take extra-mural classes at the University of London. She had never had any further education and had found herself wanting to learn again. She had started with History, moving on to Politics and Economics, then French, Spanish, Art, History and Anthropology. By the time Stephen left for university himself Anna had moved on to what was to become her true vocation: Psychology or the wherefores and hows of the human mind.

"What are you reading?" Stephen asked after he had breathed in and out a few times.

"Ernest Jones," Anna replied.

"Who?"

"Freud's biographer, another psychoanalyst. They say he was discredited."

"Discredited?"

"He slept with his patients."

Stephen laughed.

Later that night Stephen woke up and, feeling very hot, got up to open the window. As he fell back into a heavy, leaden sleep he felt weighed down, almost suffocated with pleasure. The following night he dreamt that way again, coming onto a pillow, the sheets twisted around his body, the curtains blowing wide. And the night after that his body convulsed at the moment he awoke.

He got up and took his sheets down to the laundry room for the third morning running. His mother was at the kitchen table reading the same book. "You *are* fond of clean sheets, aren't you dear?" she said. Stephen did not reply. He had breakfast and then drove his mother's car to the High Street. Mina was there, opening the office on her own.

"I'd like to postpone my flight," he said.

"You'll have to pay extra."

"I don't care."

"Unless there has been a death in the family or serious illness or something like that?"

"No death. No illness."

"What was your name again?"

Stephen cleared his throat noisily. He blushed. She had forgotten his name. "It's Stephen. Stephen Smith."

"When do you want to travel now?"

"Oh, I don't know."

"I'm going in three weeks," Mina said. "You could come with me then."

Like most people, Stephen worried about sexually transmitted diseases. So did his father. Ben frequently issued half-serious, slightly confused, warnings to his sons like, "Don't do anything you wouldn't do with your mother." When Stephen was finishing his A-levels Ben was obsessed with trying to ensure that his son went on to university the next year. He was particularly worried about girls getting in the way. All this was completely alien to Stephen who fully intended to go to university – at times like this he felt far removed from his father who he thought, somewhat guiltily, was behaving like a paranoid old Jew.

"You may think I'm behaving like a paranoid old Jew," his father was saying as Stephen put on his coat, "but you shouldn't let girls get in the way of your successful career."

"What successful career?" Stephen said sighing. "I'm too young for that."

"I don't want you getting any funny ideas. There's a good play on television tonight."

"I've got to study," Stephen interrupted, attempting to end the conversation.

Girls liked Stephen, he was seen as reliable, polite and capable of sweetness, if a little unexciting. They seduced him, and he went along happily. The first time was during a summer visit to Montréal when his cousin Rachel decided she had been a virgin long enough. At her brother's barmitzvah she whispered into his ear, "Stephen, do you want to go with me?"

"Go where?" he whispered back. He was staring at Rachel's twenty-year-old sister Sarah.

"Go. You know. Have sex. Screw."

"Screw?" he said turning to look at his cousin.

"Yeah. Later, when everybody's back at our house. We can go upstairs."

"Okay," said Stephen. As his cousin moved away he wondered what he had committed himself to.

From Rachel's bedroom they could hear the party as it grew more boisterous. "I wish they'd speak English," she said, taking off her clothes. "All that Romanian gobbledygook."

"Isn't this incest?"

"I'm not your sister. We're not going to have a baby. Close your eyes, don't look at me." Stephen took off his clothes and joined Rachel under the sheet. Her skin was soft and sticky in the humidity. She pressed her body against his, Stephen did whatever seemed appropriate. They struggled with the condom that she had bought especially and for a moment, a brief moment, they fucked.

Ben's more serious speeches about women usually began with the phrase "Some girls just aren't clean." Stephen knew what "not clean" meant; his father had explained the effects of syphilis during one of their "chats" when he was younger. Ben had gone so far as to show Stephen a rather gruesome photograph from a medical journal. He took him to see Ibsen's play *Ghosts*. But even Stephen who, at that time, had only just barely been kissed, knew that syphilis was not where things were at in those days of accelerating sexual transmission. He forgave his father his innocence though and took the girls he knew to horror movies where bodies self-destructed with technicolour disease.

Ben Smith believed in the educational power of drama. He thought that the savages ("What savages?" Stephen would ask to his father's great frustration) could be tamed through Art and that Culture would rehabilitate fools. Ben was not a naïve man but to him philistinism was a disease – a transmittable one, like those he had warned his son about – and life was best viewed through metaphor. Whenever he felt a need to explain a difficult or embarrassing subject he would suggest a play that might be suitable to read or see. He was a man of the classics at heart and for the follies of love, pride and greed he would usually suggest Shakespeare, sometimes Chekhov or Molière at a pinch.

He spurned much of modern drama as lacking in morality, although he could make do with Arthur Miller.

"Well, I'm glad to hear that you intend to study for all these exams you have coming up," Ben said, his voice solemn. Feeling as though he did nothing but study, Stephen sometimes suspected his dad thought life was a play, some epic tragedy where the sons rebel against the father causing the kingdom to fall. Stephen had never been anything but dutiful. And besides, as far as he could see, there was no kingdom.

At Oxford it became clearer to Stephen that he masqueraded as an Englishman – it was a place where he felt more Jewish and more foreign than ever before. He made friends with people whom he thought of as other foreign students. He studied hard and spent his holidays abroad with his parents. Girls seduced him at parties but even by the time he finished his degree there seemed to be no one with whom he could fall in love.

When he first met Mina Stephen did not have a job yet; he had not begun to worry about what he was going to do with his life. Neither had his parents – Ben was so relieved his son had actually finished university that he had not thought any further ahead. It did not bother Stephen that his parents were paying for his trip to New York; they had worked hard, it was what they wanted. He did not find it troublesome to accept their generosity and did not feel any real guilt around his friends who were, on the whole, much poorer.

Like Mina, Stephen felt he needed to travel but, unlike Mina, he had travelled, visiting relatives throughout Europe and North America. These family outings were soon not enough. He longed to set off on his own with a bag and a camera, to see things and record them, to put his travels down on paper.

In New York Stephen did not visit any of his ancient relatives. Instead he and Mina went up in the elevator of the Empire State Building. They walked along 42nd Street late at night trying to decide which pornographic cinema to visit. In their grey hotel room with its fluorescent strip-lighting they watched the nude talk shows on cable TV.

To Stephen's surprise, Mina would not have sex with him although they shared a bed and did not wear pyjamas. She said that Stephen had to tell her about himself first – had to confess something which she was unable to guess. Stephen began by reciting his boyhood ambitions from the other side of the bed. He laid on his back trying not to touch himself and said "When I was really little I wanted to be a teacher but by the time I became a teenager I had decided to be a lawyer but my father wants me to join his business and my mother thinks psychiatry is a better option but I don't want to go back to university and I don't really like any of these ideas at all." He described his father's business and his mother's academic career and when he thought he had probably satisfied Mina's curiosity – he believed that the reason she had asked him to speak was she did not want to sleep with a complete stranger – he rolled onto his side and in her direction. The silence informed him that she was asleep.

In the morning over coffee, eggs, pancakes and hash browns, Mina explained that she knew all those things about Stephen already from the way he dressed, spoke and behaved. He would have to confess something new. They spent the day running around skyscrapers and the sights they knew from countless movies: Mina had never been to New York before. Stephen worked hard to stay calm but had an erection all day.

That night they went to bed drunk. Mina said, "Tell me something." Stephen began by confessing his sexual fantasies, what he wanted to do with Mina if and when given the chance. He could tell she was asleep even before he stopped talking. He began to feel like Scheherazade in reverse, attempting to tell the right story and bring about what he knew must be his fate.

The next morning over a breakfast of muffins, waffles and orange juice, Mina said she was not really interested in what Stephen fantasized about but was much more concerned with what he would actually do. They spent the day riding back and forth on the Staten Island ferry and practising their American accents. Mina was convincing – she could already do Brooklyn, Texas and southern California – but Stephen was hopeless. He sounded like his father, Romanian, bits of Yiddish and English all rolled into one.

Later, when they were slow-dancing somewhere dark and smoky Stephen said, "You know, sometimes I really don't feel English at all. I don't feel Romanian either. In fact sometimes I hardly feel human. I feel like I've just arrived here from nowhere and I haven't really got a clue what comes next – how to behave, how to respond to life." He stopped abruptly, feeling as though he was sounding ridiculous.

Mina pulled Stephen closer. He felt her breathing; the smell of her hair was at once familiar and strange. She looked up and he kissed her on the lips. Apparently he had said the right thing.

The cruellest thing, Harry thought as he sat in the dark, chilly flat one night after Lucy had left, was the loss of desire. In his chair in front of the television, Harry smoked cigarettes and thought about masturbating. It was humiliating, but having a stroke was humiliating, being in the hospital was humiliating, having to be taken care of was humiliating. Harry had reached the stage where he did not really mind what anyone thought of him any more. He ignored Lucy when she came to visit. Death hung about in the eaves of the roof, waiting. Harry sat in front of the television, also waiting.

In New York, Mina had her legs wrapped around Stephen. With her hands gripping his ass she pulled him forward again and again. She had pillows behind her back; she wanted Stephen to push himself as far as possible inside her.

At first Stephen thought he would not be able to stop

himself from coming even before they had taken off their clothes. He felt very hard, the skin on his cock was pulled almost too tight. Mina admired his body – he licked hers, he slid his tongue into dark places and managed not to say anything stupid. She held her body rigid when he first penetrated her; her skin felt very cool except between her legs where she felt, Stephen thought, indescribable.

In London, Harry was by himself. Lucy had not arrived yet that day. He thought about his life and felt he had accomplished nothing. He felt dissatisfaction and anger. Where was Mina these days anyway?

Falling asleep, Harry dreamed of Mina. She was coming toward him; she was naked and looked more like Lucy than usual. She had blood on her face, her hands, and there was blood spreading between her legs, on her thighs and up around her pubic hair in shapes almost like handprints. "Are you listening, Harry?" she asked.

Harry nodded in his dream and in the dim light of the room, his head moved up and down. "You can't help me now, Harry," she said. "And I can't help you."

In New York Stephen came for the first time, arcing his pelvis into Mina's, fucking her hard, then gently, then hard again. He tried to stop himself – she had not come yet – but he could not. Mina's eyes were open, her hands sliding across his wet back. He rolled off her and curled into a ball.

Harry woke, shaking his head to chase the dream away. He sat up straight. The flat was untidy; he had not noticed before. He stood and, as he stretched, he thought he saw something out of his eye, something flashing. When he turned there was nothing. Lucy would arrive soon. He wondered what was he doing allowing her to behave like she had some stake in his illness. He took a step forward, he would show her, give her a bit of the old what-for.

Stephen slept a wide open, happy, tired sleep, his arms wrapped around Mina's tight body. She stared at the ceiling. A fly crackled with electrocution as it hit the fluorescent strip-light. Mina felt her soul twist and spin as though it was trying to tear itself free. She thought of Harry. She pushed her bum into Stephen's groin; she reached around and grabbed his thigh. As he woke he found himself with another erection.

And then Harry fell. Backwards. He split his head on the table beside his chair, he broke his arm on the chair itself and fractured some ribs when he hit the floor.

In New York when Stephen began to come again, he opened his eyes and looked at Mina. She was crouched over him, her feet on either side of his hips. Her head was turned and she was staring hard in the direction of the wall as she pushed herself against him. She cried out suddenly and said she was coming and Stephen let himself go too. Her body collapsed onto his, her breasts onto his chest, as Stephen felt hot liquid travel through his cock. Mina's eyes were closed and her lips were moving. Stephen could not hear her voice but this is what she was saying: "May the earth not receive you, may the ground not consume you . . . Are you dead Harry? . . . Harry, are you dead? . . ."

*

Mina arrived back in London to find Lucy distraught – she had discovered Harry's body, she blamed herself. "He would not have wanted you to be there when he died," Mina said angrily. "It's a private thing, death. You do it by yourself."

"Well, it would have made me feel better to have been there," replied Lucy. Mina thought her mother morbid.

Ben and Anna did not know that Stephen had been to New York with a woman and, therefore, could not understand why their son had not visited their relatives. "Uncle Joseph?" Ben asked. Stephen shook his head. "Uncle Roman?" Eventually Ben exploded, shouting, "What did you do then?"

"I spent all my time in museums and art galleries," claimed Stephen, a little self-righteously. "I went to see a production of Oscar Wilde's play *Salome*."

"That should teach you a thing or two about wilfulness."

"It's a lousy play, Dad."

Back in London, Stephen expected Mina to be there with him – his new friend, his girlfriend, the person he "was with". But Mina had never been with anyone; she carried on as she always had done – discriminating, discreet, hungry. It took Stephen a little while to figure this out. And then he got very depressed.

Mina did not care if Stephen was unhappy. She had ambition; she felt boyfriends – the ones of some duration – would only hold her back by making demands, by expecting things of her. Mina liked to work late at the office; she liked to be there after everyone else had left, at home in the empty space. She had been made assistant manager and during the day hers was the busiest desk in the office. People came back to her for their holidays; she remembered them and she remembered where to find the good deals.

Mina was never in when Stephen rang her at home, always on the other line when he rang her at work. Sometimes she went out with other men; sometimes she went to parties by herself. Stephen was not in her thoughts.

One evening at a party Mina stood staring in a mirror, not happy with her own reflection. The man with whom she had been dancing was standing behind her. He pressed his body against hers; she could feel him through his underwear, his trousers, her skirt and her tights, pushing against her skin. He liked her, he wanted her, that was all that really mattered. His desire proved something to Mina. She put a hand through her hair and, without turning, led him away even though she would have liked to have done it right there.

From time to time Mina is plagued by the blackouts and dizziness of her adolescence. A kind of darkness descends upon her. She suffers small losses of memory as if a curtain has fallen between acts, she has nightmares and wakes up in places where she can not remember falling asleep. That swirling threatens to whirl her away. But then she finds somebody, a man, and through him the dizziness recedes. She always feels better afterward, she always feels proud of herself. She does not worry about her life; everything is exactly as she needs it to be.

*

On Sundays Lucy visits Harry. He is buried in a rambling Victorian cemetery that runs alongside railway tracks. As trains shunt up and down the line, passengers stare out of the dirty windows at Lucy who stands straight and still, like a plane tree, like the backbone of a cross.

"Well Harry, I told you things would not be the same . . ." Lucy speaks out loud but in fragments, as if Harry is there to read her thoughts. "The last thing Mina told me was that she was going out with a boy she had met – always some boy, some new boy. Behaves like a man, that girl," she holds up one hand as though anticipating an interruption, "after all."

Lucy stops speaking and stands staring at the ground, at the flowers she has brought Harry. She feels her life is miserable now; she does not like her friends or her neighbours, her daughter behaves like a whore, her lover is dead, dead and gone, she lives in an ugly flat in an ugly city, there is no joy any more. Lucy heaves a great sigh and turns away.

Harry lies in his grave decomposing.

In an effort to pull himself together Stephen tried to get a job but no employer would believe he wanted to work because really, when it came down to it, he did not. He wanted to lie around and moan for love.

"Best sex I ever . . ." Stephen whispered to himself at night. Stephen felt he had no one to talk to about Mina. He thought anyone else – anyone sensible – would tell him to forget her. She was just a fling, a holiday thrill. During the nights when he could not sleep, agitated by lust, he gave himself pep-talks, cheap imitations of his father's lectures. "Spread yourself around a bit – make her come after you."

Fortified by his chanting, Stephen stopped ringing Mina and almost managed to stop wishing she would ring him. He tried to concentrate on figuring out what to do with his life. There was talk of a family trip to Portugal but this was decided against for some complex reason. On Christmas Eve Stephen was feeling maudlin, lonely and sorry for himself. He rang Mina's office and, for once, she actually answered the phone. Mina was friendly; she asked if Stephen wanted to meet for a drink. He said yes, kicking himself for not having rung earlier. They arranged to see each other in a few days.

For years all Christmas had meant to Lucy was longer hours at work. With no other family around the day had never seemed that important. The high point had been Christmas Eve when Harry would drop round with presents. He and Lucy would have a drink together, for once not sending Mina out to play. Mina would sit with Harry and beg, unsuccessfully, to be allowed to open her presents early.

On the first Christmas Eve without Harry Mina went to the office party. She did not socialize with the other agents normally; she did not flirt with her boss. Mina drank too much sparkling wine too quickly. She followed her boss to the toilet – he was a solid forty-five years of age, married with three teenaged children. On the way he turned and saw Mina behind him. Stopping, he felt compelled to take her by the shoulders and kiss her. She grabbed his left hand with her teeth, biting like an animal as his right hand travelled up her skirt. They fucked in a cubicle in the men's toilet. It only took a moment.

Later, all Mina's boss could think as he stood washing the blood off his hand was that he did not know what had happened. He had never tried to seduce an employee before. He had never been injured by one either.

Mina forgot what had happened immediately. After another drink she left and went over to Lucy's. Still a bit drunk, she felt grumpy and bored by the prospect of the hours ahead. On the landing she thought she could hear Harry's voice but when she opened the door Lucy was alone, sitting in Harry's chair.

When they met after Christmas Mina took Stephen back to her flat and tied him to her bed. No one had ever tied up Stephen before. Using thick ropes she had bought the previous day, Mina tied Stephen's ankles and wrists together and then tied those ropes to the opposite ends of the bed. Then she lay still beside his body, her eyes wide open, examining his reaction.

Stephen's heart was beating so quickly he felt as though the skin on his chest must be visibly jumping up and down. He could hardly breathe from the weight of his excitement. Without looking at Mina's body he could smell her – she smelt of perfume and sex. He had never felt so powerless before, this was a new pleasure and one so very dense.

Buying the ropes had been almost as exciting as using them. Mina blindfolded Stephen and his excitement grew with his fear. She bit his nipples, she nipped his cock with her teeth. He could hear her breath catch in her throat and then the next thing he felt was her fucking him. She pushed his shoulders down with her hands and moved hard, back and forth, up and down. Stephen felt he himself was being penetrated and as he came he lost control, his mind went somewhere else. He left his body to Mina and did not think about what she would do with it next.

Mina does not want to hurt Stephen; she knows he does not really want to be hurt. But there is something in the way he holds his body when he speaks that makes Mina think she can do anything to him. She sees he can admit to wanting these things, he can allow her to see. For Mina that is enough for the time being; for Stephen it is the start of something, of what he has no idea.

Again Stephen's expectations were unfulfilled, again he had to fight to forget Mina. It was not as though he did not know where to find her – he knew where she worked and now he knew where she lived – but he was not about to go and seek her out and pound on the door until she let him in. A few unanswered phonecalls, one missed date: that was enough to give Stephen the shove.

Mina was amazed by Stephen's lack of persistence and, in her way, pleased about it. Once she realized he was going to be a bit more than a holiday romance it felt important that he was not too insistent. He seemed the kind of man who would understand Mina's own brand of blind drive without having much of it himself. It was to Mina's advantage that he was easy to dump. She never had to push him too hard.

Harry had been naturally heartless. He thought of himself as big-hearted which meant he needed more than one woman to keep his heart happy. He did not care how his women felt when he was not around and they always seemed happy enough when he was.

Mina's heartlessness is calculated, it is something she works hard at. She does not compare herself to Harry. As far as she is concerned he was an old man who died, stupidly, of a stroke, weak and sick in the end, smaller than he had been in real life. Mina never understood what Harry saw in her mother. She does not see Harry in herself.

Despite his age, Stephen is still a little afraid of the dark.

He does not like to let his feet dangle off the end of the bed, he does not like to open his eyes when he is alone in his room late at night. When he reads frightening novels – he likes Stephen King but keeps this a secret – he places the book underneath a piece of clothing when he is not reading it. Stephen is not afraid of being robbed or attacked when out late at night in the streets of London, he is much more concerned with the awful things that might happen to him at home.

These fears do not plague Stephen to the extent that his daily life is full of things to be avoided. In fact, he has these attacks of fearfulness fairly infrequently, only when he is lonely, and, recently, only when he has been with Mina.

Stephen moped around his parents' house like a teenager. He sat down at his old desk with a pen and some paper and wished he had someone to whom to write. He started thinking about the trip to New York. He made a list of all the places he and Mina had visited, trying to remember sights, smells. After a few hours he began to write a description of the trip. He left out the sex but, when finished, the piece still contained a degree of sauciness he found appealing. The next day he sent the article to a local newspaper and, much to his surprise, the editor rang at the end of the week and said he would like to use it. Ben and Anna were so pleased and impressed that they took their son out to dinner after buying him a suit. They drank champagne. Stephen felt he had discovered what he was going to do. He would be all right now, he thought, reassured by success; Mina could just fade away.

Mina moved jobs; she was given a better position at a bigger and more aggressive travel agency. She was becoming an expert on the sunny places of southern Europe and was frequently sent on reconnaissance trips to resorts on the Mediterranean. She managed a department, had a staff of three and spent a lot of money getting her clothes right. The way she dressed had to suit the person she wanted people to see. She wore red lipstick which made her teeth look white and strong like an American's – they shone when she smiled. She bought a flat, not far from her mum.

Lucy was not promoted to manager of her shop; the head office kept her at assistant manager level and appointed a man who was both younger and less senior than her. Mina took a drink from a glass of water and spat into the kitchen sink when she heard this.

"What do you mean, you don't mind?"

"Oh, all that added responsibility would be too much for me."

"As far as I can see you've been managing that stupid shop for the last ten years anyway."

"They need a man," Lucy said tentatively, "to keep control of things. You know, inflation and everything."

Mina took another gulp and spat again as though trying to wash out her mouth. "You can't let everybody step on you, Mum, you should be more assertive."

"Stop spitting then. What's all this spitting anyway? Very unladylike."

"I've got this awful taste down the back of my throat," Mina said. "I woke up with it this morning."

That same morning Stephen woke to find his sheets soaked as though he had had wet dream after wet dream in the night. In the evening he put on his new suit and went out for a walk telling Anna, immersed in Lacan, that he would not be long. He walked down the high street and stopped in at a pub. As he ordered his drink, he turned to find Mina standing beside him.

"Hi," she said, friendly.

"Hello," Stephen said, shocked. He looked at his feet.

"Can I buy you a drink?"

Stephen looked up about to say no. He was angry with Mina and he wanted to stay angry. He wanted to be the one to do the pushing away this time but something in Mina's eyes caught him. He felt frozen, as if she had dipped him through a hole in an iced-over sea. "Okay," he said, his voice brittle.

And Stephen was still there, lurking near the door when Mina came back from the bar. She was wearing a red polka dot dress and it seemed incongruous on her body, as girlish and carefree as she was not. They had several drinks. Mina played her favourite records on the jukebox, old Country and Western songs, "Stand By Your Man" and "Ring of Fire". Stephen drank beer,

Mina drank gin and tonic. They left the pub at closing time.

Later, Stephen could not recall what they talked about that evening. He walked Mina home, stumbling and trying to make a comedy out of his desire. Outside the front door of her flat, Mina slid her arms around Stephen's waist and kissed him. He leaned back against the wall as she undid his trousers. Stephen closed his eyes as Mina slid down onto her knees. "You don't have to do that," he thought. But the only sound he made was the release of his breath. He put his hands in her hair as she pushed her forehead against his pubic bone. They could easily be caught; it was not that late. But instead of objecting Stephen pushed himself deep into Mina's throat, only making a sound when he came. Mina stood, put her arms around Stephen and held him tight. Very tight, he thought, dimly, as he leaned into her. He didn't feel anything at all for a moment, until Mina stepped away, wiping her mouth with the back of her hand. And then suddenly he felt very tired.

Mina left Stephen leaning against the wall. She opened her front door, stepped in and was gone. When he tried to, Stephen could not remember what he had done next, how he got home that night, in what state or at what time. It was as though she had anaesthetized him.

At the earliest indication that Mina was about to disappear Stephen would buy himself a ticket and leave London. Sometimes he stayed in Britain, seeking out quiet villages and busy market towns; on other occasions he travelled abroad but never too far or anywhere too distant and strange. Apart from Cairo and, once, Morocco, he stayed in Europe. It was almost as though his life in London provided him with enough adventure. He travelled to come to terms with himself; he travelled to be reassured by the ordered, daily patterns of life elsewhere.

For both Mina and Stephen travel was an experience simultaneously immediate and distancing, involved and detached. Without a common language Mina felt she never needed to explain anything to anyone; to communicate she waved her hands, pointed at menus, and made sure her desires showed up clearly across her face. Working in the industry made her feel she had unlimited access to Europe, she liked knowing she could fly to Paris on a whim.

For Stephen, travel writing made work out of running away. He liked to be out on the streets when he travelled. He liked to look at things and attempt to understand them, to be moved by a city or a country, and then travel on somewhere new. Travel made him feel a part of the world. If he felt an unnatural outsider at home at least abroad he would feel naturally alien – no one expected him to fit in.

Sometimes Stephen and Mina would not meet for a week, sometimes much longer but, whatever the length of time, to Stephen it always felt like forever. He alternated between everlasting devotion and end-of-the-affair dejection like a weathervane, turning as the wind blew. There was no discernible pattern to their relationship, often there was no discernible relationship.

When they did meet Stephen tried hard to play it cool, to be nonchalant, noncommital. But Mina undermined him every time – they always ended up having sex. They ran around the city looking for alleyways to entice each other into; they fucked with a fury that could easily have been anger; they made each other stiff, bruised and raw with passion. In the morning Stephen would wake with a mouthful of expectations which he would have to struggle to swallow over the following days.

Stephen tried to console himself by thinking that Mina kept rejecting him because he was getting to her, touching something she did not want to be touched. However most of the time he felt used and discarded, like a condom, a soiled tissue or dirty sheets in a pile on the floor.

Of course Stephen wondered what Mina did when not seeing him but without playing the role of some sort of private detective he could not think of any way to find out. Stephen was not a private eye kind of a man.

"So. What have you been up to?"

"Nothing." End of conversation; he could see it in the way she held her lips.

"So, Mina," another time, "why did you disappear suddenly? Something come up at work?"

"No."

She could not be pinned down, she could not be

taken, she would not allow herself to be known. For Stephen this was endlessly frustrating; it was endlessly intriguing as well.

And so they were on again, off again, and then on one more time. Stephen could not help himself – she was there, already she was all he wanted. They were meeting very regularly now, every night when Mina finished work, always staying at her flat. On the weekend they bought several bottles of wine and locked themselves in.

"You've cut yourself," Mina said. She was sitting on the edge of the bath watching Stephen shave. "On your neck, towards your ear." Stephen stretched his head back, washed the blood away and continued with his task. He concentrated, making shaving faces, flattening his upper lip, pulling one cheek taut, then the other. He liked being watched by Mina. It made him feel like a craftsman.

"You're still bleeding," she said, standing. Mina was wearing a large towel, Stephen was in his underwear. "I hate to see you bleed." She stood behind him and ran her hands up and down his back.

"Me too," said Stephen dabbing the blood away. Mina began to kiss his back. "I'll just put a bit of toilet paper on it," he said, "like men do in the movies."

Mina slid her hands down into the front of his underwear. He could feel her body had become hot as if she had suddenly developed a temperature. She pulled his underwear down in one quick movement. "Ooh," he said, "I'm being attacked."

On the second weekend when Stephen went home to fetch clean clothes, Ben began shouting before his son had opened the front door. "What do you think this is, some kind of doss house? Who do you think we are, hoteliers? If you think you can waltz in and out of here, reeking of booze, and . . . and . . . dissolution, well you're wrong. No son of mine –"

Anna interrupted. "Hello Stephen. How are you?"

"I'm fine Mum," said Stephen as he stared at his father whose face had turned heart-attack red.

"Why don't you bring her to dinner tomorrow night? Joseph is bringing Susan round."

"Okay."

"Who's 'HER'?" shouted Ben.

"Mina. She's a travel agent," replied Stephen.

"A TRAVEL AGENT?"

"Yes."

"Leave those Stephen," Anna said, pointing at his bag of laundry. "I'll do them for you."

Even though Mina did not like to admit it, or even think about it too much, something was happening between her and Stephen. She was getting used to him. She liked his body, she liked his face; he always seemed to know just what to do. He would not be too much trouble, she thought. She could keep him under control. She could keep him close, within reach, just an arm's length away.

Stephen had something that she liked although she did not know what this was. "Maybe," she thought, "maybe it's just the way he smells."

Mina had never been invited to a boyfriend's house before. Automatically she assumed it was Stephen's father who would be hardest to impress so she wore a tight dress and high heels and spent a long time on her face. They went by cab to the Smith house.

At dinner Stephen's brother, Joseph, told loud stories about his life as a stockbroker in the City. He and Stephen argued about the ethics of investment banking. Anna asked Mina quiet, friendly questions about what she did, requesting travel advice. Ben drank a lot and tried not to stare at his son's girlfriend. Joseph's girlfriend, Susan, attempted to distract Ben, remembering how he had grilled her the first time Joseph brought her to the house. But Ben would not be distracted. Inside his head contradictions waged war; she was sexy therefore sluttish and his son was too good for her; how had Stephen ever got his hands on such a good-looking woman?; she was attractive therefore she must be a bit silly; what did a successful business woman see in his dreamy unambitious son?; she was of the wrong class and religion but she spoke well, despite her accent, and had much better manners than his son.

By the end of the meal, Ben was ready to recite passages from *Romeo and Juliet* but Stephen saw this coming and pre-empted it by suggesting he show Mina the garden. "In the dark?" asked Ben loudly as they went out the door.

Outside the house Stephen kissed Mina. "They're nice," she said, running her hand inside his shirt. "Nice family people," she added as if this was something new to her. Stephen pulled up her dress. "We mustn't be out here too long," he said between kisses.

That night in bed in her flat Mina was passionate and solicitous and, later, she was coy, almost demure, as she persuaded Stephen to fuck her, like he did not care how it felt to her, like all he wanted was to make himself come right up inside her, as deep as he could get.

After the evening with his parents Stephen almost expected Mina to disappear, although his lack of surprise did not stop him from feeling desperate. Her absence made him feel incomplete but somehow her presence did as well. Stephen had to get himself together. He could no longer be the idle artistic wastrel his father had him marked down as being. "If I am going to be a wastrel I'll do it on my own terms," he shouted one day when Ben had attached too many conditions to his handout. Besides, Stephen admired the way Mina was devoted to hard graft and getting ahead. Gradually he was beginning to find his father's patronage offensive. He did not make much money but he thought he might be able to make enough to pay his own rent. So he packed his possessions – plus a few of his parents' – and moved out.

Although rapidly becoming something of an expert on how to travel inexpensively, Stephen was not an expert on how to find a cheap flat in London. He ended up with a couple of grimy rooms above a newsagent on the same street as Mina's old travel agency – he felt happy being near even though she no longer worked there. The cheques his father continued to present to him on birthdays, Christmas, Channukah, Yom Kippur, Easter etc. stopped annoying him. He began to make more money, to write more about where he travelled, from different angles. The local newspaper gave him a column called "Cheap Destination of the Week" and he began to sell pieces to the national papers. Stephen thrived, Ben's cheques piled up uncashed. Stephen pinned them on his wall – they mocked him and he mocked them back.

Mina thought a lot about the evening she spent at the Smith's and had surprised herself by realizing how much she enjoyed it. Stephen's family seemed chaotic, self-absorbed and contradictory, everyone opinionated, his mother kind. She found herself wondering if they liked her.

Mina thinks that if Stephen knows her any better he will not want to know her any more.

Mina is afraid although she always seems very brave; she is afraid that Stephen will try to tell her how to live. She worries he will judge her. But more than that she fears seeing the details of her life laid out – she does not want to be watched. It is as though she fears discovery in a trial; the evidence against her will be revealed.

Mina lives as though she has something to hide.

Stephen was not surprised that Mina rarely spoke about her past. He knew that she and her mother had lived alone. She had never mentioned Harry; like Lucy she was uncomfortable speaking about herself. Stephen learned about Mina by what she did not say.

And Mina listened as Stephen talked, telling her his history in bits and pieces. "This is the story of my life," he could have said. "I'm giving it to you for safe-keeping." By talking he made himself feel real; by saying "I am this-this-and-this," he could convince himself he actually was all those things. When Stephen touched Mina's body he sometimes thought "*I* am touching *her*," as though that formed a Cartesian equation. Mina's unflinching sexual confidence made him feel more substantial; it was a simple fact that when they fucked he felt more alive.

For Mina there were no equations like this. Being with Stephen made her feel she had ballast, but that ballast needed to be thrown overboard from time to time. Sex for her was also revelatory but in an opposite way. When she and Stephen fucked Mina felt herself become less substantial – she felt herself become part of him. Something gave way. It was this that was frightening, even threatening. But part of her liked this feeling as well.

Another month apart and then Mina was back, ringing

Stephen, calling out his name in the midst of passion. They made love outdoors, upsetting the ducks in St James's Park at two in the morning. Mina liked to go into the grounds of an old church near her flat. The parish had moved all the gravestones to one side in order to create a more usable green space; it had become a place where during the day office workers dropped litter while eating their lunches and children wearing rollerskates fought on the footpath. At night the row of tombstones looked like bared teeth; Mina liked to bite Stephen's nipples in the shadows of the church, beneath the flying buttresses.

In one of her sporadic attempts to be normal, Mina invited Stephen to come to dinner to meet Lucy. Stephen was extremely pleased by this invitation; Mina was nervous. Lucy was very surprised.

"You want me to come to dinner to meet your boyfriend?"

"Yes. About 7:00."

"Shouldn't I come at 6:00 and help you cook?"

"No, I've got it all planned. It will be fine."

Stephen arrived just after seven. Mina came to the door wearing an apron. He laughed out loud.

"Don't laugh," she said. "I take entertaining at home very seriously." So seriously she had never done it before, but she did not say that. Stephen followed her through to the sitting room. Mina lived in a small ground floor flat in a row of terraced houses. She had a garden which she neglected and a kitchen in which the only noticeable feature was a coffee machine. Lucy was standing by the sink staring in the mirror. She had just noticed a new streak of grey in her hair. Mina led Stephen in.

"This is my mother. Mum, this is Stephen." The kitchen was far too small for three; Mina stepped forward and Lucy and Stephen moved into the corridor.

"Hello, Mrs Savage," Stephen said, holding out his hand.

"Miss. But call me Lucy."

"Lucy. Call me Stephen," he said awkwardly. There was a brief silence during which Mina banged some pots together. "Mina tells me you live nearby?"

"Yes. Only a five or ten minute walk. Mina grew up there, in fact I've always lived there. And where do you live?"

"Not far. Not far at all."

"And, do you have a job?" Lucy was trying to be tactful. Later she would have a sore neck from holding herself so upright.

"Well, I work freelance."

"Oh, freelance," said Lucy nodding.

"Yes, I write travel articles for newspapers and magazines."

"Travel," Lucy nodded again. "Like Mina. Is that how you met?"

"Yes, in her old office. We – she – yes, in her old office." Stephen's head began to hurt. Lucy was smaller than her daughter, plainer; they did not look much alike. Lucy's past was already imprinted on her face. Work had moulded her; loneliness had stiffened her into shape.

Mina came into the room and offered them both drinks which Stephen said he would fetch. Lucy stared at the floor while trying to think of something to say. Mina sat down beside her mother as Stephen handed her a glass. She began to talk about a brand-new hotel on the French Riviera where her company had recently sent her. The others asked questions and, for a while, everything seemed okay. Then Mina served dinner with Lucy's help – it came from packets which Mina had warmed in the oven. Everything she served came from packets; even the salad was pre-chopped.

"Do you travel?" Stephen asked Lucy while they ate.

"No," said Lucy, reddening.

"Mum has never been outside of the country . . ." Mina stopped speaking suddenly, not wanting to embarrass her mother. It was as though the conversation had been beheaded. From that point on it refused to come back to life. Out of desperation Lucy asked Stephen what he had done at Christmas. Mina looked at her mother in alarm. Stephen, flustered, felt he needed to come clean. "I'm Jewish," he said abruptly.

"No Christmas?" Lucy asked, nodding her head.

"Not really," Stephen said, also nodding.

Mina spoke without nodding. "Well we're hardly believers ourselves, are we, Mum?" Later they would all wonder what had happened. Lucy knew other Jewish people, it was not as if she had never heard of people who did not have Christmas. She felt she must have looked stupid. Stephen wondered why he had suddenly blurted this confession when his family did celebrate Christmas, in fact probably more elaborately than Lucy and Mina themselves. He felt he must have appeared to be trying to make a point. Mina felt cross with her mother and cross with Stephen as well. She wished they would both leave.

Which, eventually, they did. Lucy left because she had to get in to work early the next day, Stephen because he did not want to embarrass Lucy further by hanging around as though he intended to stay the night with her daughter. They left at the same time and walked in opposite directions. While doing the washing-up, Mina smashed a plate, slicing her hand while trying to fish the pieces out of the sink.

Later, Lucy and Stephen sat in their flats looking out of their windows at the night. It was windy and clouds passed over the moon as though on fast forward. They both felt sad; they considered how alone the dark made them feel.

Mina lay in bed feeling dizzy. Her hand throbbed where she had cut it. She sat up and held her head as though that would still what she felt inside. Her bedroom window was closed, she wanted it to be open. She swung her bare legs out from beneath the covers and stood, stretching her arms. Then she walked towards the window silently.

*

The decision to go away on holiday together had not

been an easy one. "Please," Stephen said on more than one occasion. "No," Mina replied. To Stephen the idea of a holiday seemed gloriously radical – if he got her away on her own it would mean no-holds-barred romance. He would get to be with her all day every day. Mina, however, associated taking planes and going places with work and being alone. She was worried that she would reveal too much of herself, that Stephen's desire for her would not withstand such close, continual contact, that he might discover something about her which he did not like.

"I'll organize all the practical things," Stephen pleaded. "You won't have to make any decisions or hotel reservations or anything." He always talked to her about his plans immediately after or even while they had sex because this was when they were both at their most agreeable. "Imagine we are lying on a beach," he would whisper while fucking her, "imagine we are in a room in an expensive hotel." Slowly but surely he broke down her resolve.

Spain allowed them to be both indolent and expansive. There was a certain clarity in the air, it made life sharper, more keen. They were both so accustomed to travelling alone that they had to spend great chunks of the day negotiating their plans; the trip to New York seemed from a past life. Their needs and desires usually coincided although sometimes they felt obliged to oppose each other, just to make a point.

"No, no, I'm not hungry yet," Stephen would say.

"We have to do it like they do in Spain, you know, like real people do."

"People should eat whenever they feel like it."

"Well we are not on the costa now sweetheart."

"Well we are not on the costa now sweetheart," Mina would repeat through clenched teeth.

They were travelling by hired car, stopping at roadside cafés for long lunches, searching for hidden rivers to cool off in. The heat was epic and their laziness was as monumental as their appetites. The arid and eucalyptus-scented Spanish countryside stretched ahead as they drove through the rocky hills, leaving the sea behind. Stephen imagined their holiday had a soundrack. He whistled the theme music from *The Good, The Bad and The Ugly* behind the steering wheel, exclaiming in Spanish whenever they passed another of the enormous wooden black bulls that stand against the sky, advertisements for some kind of sherry or brandy.

They wanted to be in the cities at night, amidst the crowded bars and shops. In the evenings they went to restaurants where they sat at tables next to fountains and ate red soup and white fish and fried aubergines. They stayed out late in Granada, later in Cordoba, and much, much later still in Seville. Stephen wanted to drink what the locals drank; Mina stuck to gin and tonic. "You can always tell that you're really enjoying a place," Stephen said, "when you want to immigrate." Mina worked hard to stop herself from eating *churros*, oily strips of fried dough dipped in thick hot chocolate. Stephen ate platefuls whenever given the chance, his enjoyment intensified by the greedy way Mina watched him. He liked doing something she could not.

Stephen found it easy to make Mina laugh – for once he felt he could say whatever he wanted. In London he felt Mina was always only a few inches away from leaving him but in Spain the gap between them narrowed to the space between their bodies when they slept. And they slept together every night. Every night as the moon waned and then disappeared altogether they slept as though they were married and always would be. They stayed in rooms with balconies overlooking narrow streets and noisy bars. They left shutters and windows open as they got into bed, feeling drunk and full and warm as they made love, overheard by the people in the next room. After one week Mina began to wear Stephen's clothes.

This was a process which neither of them had been through before. It reminded them of nothing – no better holidays, no other lovers who did things differently. Together they felt very young and excitable, playing at being adult, playing at being away on holiday. Their needs became basic: food, drink, sex and a bit of scenery. They spent a lot of time in the car; its upholstery began to smell like their skin.

But while Stephen grew verbose, telling more and more elaborate stories about his past, Mina still remained silent on most subjects concerning herself. They talked about sex quite a lot and, of course, they discussed what they were seeing as they travelled.

"This is what I miss most when I travel alone,"

Stephen said. "Having someone to point things out to."

"I thought you liked travelling alone – you always say it's a good way to meet people."

"I don't need to meet anyone, Mina. I've got you."

In the mornings they drank large coffees and ate *tostadas* soaked in olive oil and pepper. One day Stephen bought an English newspaper before breakfast. They had not thought about the real world since they arrived. Absolutely anything could have happened at home: a plane crash, a train crash, a fire in the Underground, a ferry lost at sea. Stephen paid four times as much as he would for the same paper in London.

"You shouldn't have bought it," Mina said, "it reminds me of home and work and everything."

"We will have to go back eventually you know."

"Why remind me when I'm having a nice time?" She is right, Stephen thought. If we were at home she would leave me again.

Four-star hotels with their swimming pools and mini-bars proved too tempting to resist. They abandoned their economy travel guide by the side of the road one day. As he parked the car Stephen told himself he could make the money back by writing about spending it; Mina reasoned that this was the first real holiday she had ever taken. Credit cards made luxury easy. For both of them these hotels invited anonymity: they liked being nothing but a name and room number, it made them feel like adulterers. She wore earrings in the pool and swam without getting her hair wet. He bought a white bathrobe and wore his dark glasses in the lift. They got drunk at lunchtime and had slow, sweaty, afternoon sex.

One day while Stephen slept, Mina got up and went back down to the pool by herself. Her feet propped on a lounge chair in the hot sun, she felt the skin between the straps of her sandals burn. She would be carried back to London on feet criss-crossed with tan. A man with a herd of goats walked just beyond the edge of the hotel's garden; the goats were multicoloured, brown, black, white and grey. One of the animals paused to look at Mina sitting on the terrace sipping beer. She looked down at herself. Sometimes wearing a bathing suit seemed worse than having to wander around naked.

Even now, absorbed and absolved by Stephen's passion as he gave her endless proof that he wanted her, that he found her unbearably attractive, Mina did not like her own body. She wanted to be flat and solid like a board with a cross-bar for shoulders. She wanted smooth rounded stones for breasts and thighs like steel plates, absolute in their firmness. She wanted to be everything she was not, to have a body like Stephen's, angular and thin with no surprises. As she was growing older this ideal was slowly becoming less obtainable and Mina found she desired it all the more.

Then one night Stephen woke to find Mina sitting upright in bed. He said her name out loud into the silent night, touching her shoulder. "Mina. Wake up." She turned and looked down, her eyes glinting in the dim light. He realized she was still not awake. When he pulled her body toward his she did not resist.

In the morning Mina said she had had a bad dream but refused to give Stephen any details. She looked pale beneath her tan. That night Stephen woke again and found Mina standing beside the bed. He got up and took her by the shoulders. "Mina. Wake up." Again she slowly turned to look at him and then allowed him to guide her back into the bed. But when she did not respond to Stephen's caresses he fell back asleep.

Mina dreams she is trapped in a hotel room. Stephen is there with her but he is dead. No one has entered and no one has left. Stephen is naked; his blood is on the walls. All Mina wants to do is leave, get away from this appalling scene.

In the morning Mina would still not talk about what was disturbing her sleep. Stephen was hurt: now there were things they did not share. He wanted everything of Mina's to be his; he wanted to give everything of his to her.

"That is love," Stephen said, emphatic.

"That's impossible," Mina replied. She spent the whole day seated at a table in a square, fending off beggars with a lazy flick of her hand while Stephen, stubborn and conscientous, visited two museums and an art gallery. He was lucky he was not there to witness Mina's daring. She flirted with the waiter who brought her coffee. She smiled at the young Spanish man at the next table. He came over to sit with her under the large umbrella. They laughed as Mina practised her Spanish.

Stephen was not there to hear as the young man taught her how to say "I love you". The Spanish words tripped lightly off her tongue. She said it again in German, in French, then Italian. I love you. I love you. I love you. The young man told her he loved her in Portuguese. These were words Stephen and Mina had never exchanged in any language.

Mina and the stranger giggled. Then he got up to go back to work. He explained where he would like Mina to meet him later so he could take her for drinks and show her around. Stephen was lucky that Mina's Spanish had not improved that much.

They argued again later that day. "There is absolutely nothing wrong with going somewhere to lie on the beach, go to discos, drink beer and have a good time," Mina said. "Who cares if they don't try to speak Spanish; who cares if they don't like Spanish food? The Spanish are happy as long as the hotels are full."

"But they are missing so much in the way of Art and History . . . it's arrogant and boorish and rude . . ."

"Who gives a fuck? It's a holiday."

That evening Stephen got very drunk. Mina seemed distant and vague, she hardly spoke. They were in a cave-like bodega where a woman fried mountains of fish over an open fire. The waiter told Stephen – he imagined he had understood every word – that the bar had been a hide-out for anarchists during the Civil War. With each glass of wine this notion brought Stephen closer to tears. "Those were the days," he sighed. Mina ignored him.

Stephen made friends with the Italians at the next table. He shouted to them in broken Italian about what a great country they came from, how they make great movies and write great books and have beautiful cities and wonderful food and what a shame it was about Mussolini and the Mafia. They shouted back at him in bad English about London, football and Princess Diana. They ordered more beer and made multi-lingual jokes.

Mina was in another world, almost, except the real world kept impinging, getting in her way, like a glaring light when she longed for darkness. It was as though her body contained a powerful storm which she felt beginning to stir. A small part of her wished this swirling would go away but another part, the bigger part, was desperate to give in.

That night they went to bed late. Stephen's blood ran slowly, syrupy with alcohol, thick like his tongue. He was too drunk to fuck, but Mina was not interested anyway. He fell into a deep sleep.

In the middle of the night, which was dark and muggy with the heat, Stephen awoke. His head felt clotted, his spine gnarled. He reached out a stiff arm. Mina was gone.

A coolish breeze floated in through the open window. With effort Stephen made himself conclude that Mina must be in the toilet – where else could she be? He withdrew his leaden hand, rolled over and went back to sleep.

In the morning Mina was vivid and bright. She pestered

Stephen awake, moving her fingers up and down his stomach, one hand loosely around his half-erect prick. Stephen moaned and thought he might throw-up but Mina was insistent and although most of him felt dead, part of him responded. "Oh leave me alone," he moaned again halfheartedly.

"Relax," said Mina. She put a pillow over his head. Now the world was muffled and Stephen felt a bit better. He heard Mina's voice through the feathers and cloth. "This will make you feel better." He felt her lips, then her tongue on his cock. Fighting back nausea he laid still. Eventually Mina began to fuck him. Under the pillow, which she now held down on either side, he felt happily abused. He let himself be taken over.

She lifted the pillow off his face and gave it to him to hug. He was asleep again almost immediately. Mina got up, pulled on a dress and walked to the bathroom. She studied herself in the mirror. Where yesterday she seemed to be sagging today she looked taut. She bit her lips; they were red. She went down into the street to a café.

Eventually Stephen's hangover left him and they picked up their holiday where they had deserted it. The time to leave came too soon. They spent the few hours of the plane's inevitable delay at a restaurant on the beach sampling different kinds of fish. A short flight and then they were back in London where they took a train, and then a cab before they separated. It was over as suddenly as it began.

*

But again, although now they are bound by much more than sex, by the undeniable accumulation of shared experience, Mina can not cope with Stephen's bare-faced devotion. She is unwilling to give anything more than what she has already. Stephen's love is like a black hole to Mina, a vast unknown entity into which she must try not to fall. For much of the time Mina feels she is beyond love.

Stephen is much less easy to shave off than before. There is an ugly tension between them; Stephen storms off and then storms back again. He slams down the telephone when Mina doesn't answer it – he is shocked to realize that he still doesn't know what she is thinking. He loves her, that is straightforward enough. But nothing else holds any clarity.

Stephen searches his memory for clues, fed up with being understanding. Is there someone else, are there others? And now that he has started wondering, he can't stop. If there are others, does she take risks? Is she endangering him? How can he continue to live with Mina's inconstancy? It's like something his father would have warned him about.

"You are using your fear of disease to try to force me to be less independent . . ."

"Damn right I am."

"But you can't do that, Stephen. It doesn't work like that."

Finally Mina shuts the door of her flat in his face one evening; Stephen goes home, unloved again.

*

So Stephen attempted celibacy. He did not say anything to Mina; he simply decided he would have to stop seeing her. Stephen tried to organize his life so that he was out of town when Mina was in. Celibacy was an odd notion, more a state of mind than anything else. He was alone a lot of the time anyway; he and Mina had always been together less than they were apart. At first it seemed novel. He longed to be able to say "Sorry, I'm celibate" to a woman at a party but, of course, the opportunity did not arise. He ached just as badly and felt just as randy. Eventually he began to find the idea itself depressing – he was too young to feel so spinsterish. He started spending more time at home with his parents, hoping they might cheer him up. And, in a way, they did. He did not talk to them about Mina, in fact he didn't really talk to them about anything at all. He watched TV with Ben and ate his mother's dinners – they were happy to have him there.

Ben worried about Stephen. He knew that Mina was often away and thought that his son might "feel lonely" at times. One day Stephen found himself in his father's car listening to a vaguely familiar lecture.

"Ibsen just won't do these days, Dad," he interrupted. "It's not nineteenth-century Norway and I'm not going to get syphilis." Ben had anticipated this reaction from his son. He reached over, opened the glove compartment of the new car, and pulled out a box of condoms.

"You keep large boxes of Durex in your glovebox?"

"I bought them for you," Ben said, alarmed.

"Oh, so do you and mum have safe sex then?"

Lucy felt it was time to end her graveside visits to Harry. She told herself that Harry would not mind although, of course, he did.

"Harry," she said out loud after putting down the flowers one final Sunday, "the girl is just like you. She's arrogant and she won't let anybody help her. She's got desires too big for her own good. I certainly can't get through to her." After a few moments Lucy turned and walked away, her thoughts no longer with Harry. She ignored the wind that passed overhead carrying his words of wisdom. "She is not in control," the breeze said. "No one is."

Always alone at night now, Stephen began to see things out of the corner of his eye, after midnight when the city was dark and still. He was forever sitting at his desk, standing by the sink or walking towards a door, and seeing something move just there, barely beyond the broad sweep of his vision, just behind him to the left or the right. A quick little movement, then he would turn and it would be gone, like a small animal, a crisp wrapper in a breeze, a departing foot. This happened with enough frequency to become imbued with *déjà vu*; Stephen would be momentarily overcome with terror. He would think to himself, "What is it? I am not prepared." But then these thoughts would disappear and Stephen forgot until it happened again.

Without seeing each other, Mina and Stephen spoke often on the telephone, Stephen allowed himself that.

They were both travelling a lot and their schedules conflicted quite naturally. He rang her from Whitby one day. She rang him between meetings. Stephen hid his feelings well and it took a bit of time for Mina to guess that he was avoiding her.

She was having a drink with a man she had just met, the managing director of the resort where she was staying. He was telling her about how his wife insisted on arranging to be away when he was at home.

"It's as though we're divorced already," he said. "We've certainly got the custody arrangements well worked out."

Mina nodded and flashed her "I understand" smile. Then she paled slightly, thinking of Stephen.

"Are you married?"

"Oh," she said, "no," her mind somersaulting. She returned her focus back to the man. He had something she wanted.

Later Mina lay awake thinking about Stephen. She had never taken him and his threats very seriously before. He had always been there when she needed him – it suited her to believe that they both liked things that way. She liked having him available to her, she liked having him around. She thought the arguments they had had in the past about how much to see each other were part of a process of negotiation. She needed lots of time to herself; he had to understand that. But since the trip to Spain it had been more difficult for both of them: she suddenly wanted to see him again.

Mina returned home from her trip early. Stephen was

leaving London the next day. He was ironing a shirt as she knocked on the door. When he opened it she was standing there smiling. There was not a lot he could do to resist.

That night Stephen spoke as they were falling asleep. "Mina," he said, "can't we see each other more regularly? I need to be able to trust you, I need to feel . . ."

"I don't know," she replied. "Will it make you happy?"

"Yes."

"Will you let me see you when I want to see you and then leave me alone sometimes?"

"Yes. We could go away together more often."

Mina was silent.

"Can't you try?" Stephen asked.

"Okay, I'll try," she replied.

"Promise?"

"All right. I'll try."

Mina had never promised anyone anything before. She made herself promises all the time; she promised herself to work harder, to spend less money, to take better care of herself, to get more sleep especially when she was having dizzy spells. She had never tried promising to stay away from strange men, and she knew that this was what Stephen was really asking.

Mina was not optimistic about her first attempt at keeping a promise but she could tell Stephen was serious and she had weighed her options carefully. The scale came down on Stephen's side, at least for the time being.

Stephen knew that in a sense lovers are like parasites; they prey upon each other in the worst kind of way. When one is strong, the other is weak. Sometimes these roles alternate. Monogamy involves a concentration of this feeding process; each partner is responsible for surviving the other's appetite.

When Stephen asked Mina to stop seeing other men he knew he was asking her to concentrate all her swirling energy on him. He also knew there was a chance he could not stand up to this: there was always the threat that the intensity would prove too much for him or even, more simply, that Mina would be bored.

Mina knew that Stephen failed to understand that it was not a simple question of her giving up sex with other men – she had other, stronger needs, other desires. He thought her self-image relied upon the desire of others to keep itself intact; but Mina was more complicated than that.

"Does it feel good?" he asked his reflection. He watched himself in the mirror, Mina was bending too low to be seen.

'Yes."

"Do you want me?"

"Yes."

"Do you need me inside you?"

"Yes." These were the questions Stephen felt compelled to ask. He asked them incessantly.

"Do I make you excited? Do you want me, Mina, do you?"

"Yes."

Stephen fucked Mina harder. She bent lower still.

And what Stephen begins to feel he needs to survive is this; what it comes down to in the end as far as Mina is concerned is this; where all conversations, entertainments, light touches and smiles, all meals and drinks, confidences, stories and walks, taxi rides and telephone calls lead; where each trust is gained, intimacy shared and promise made; what it all leads to is this:
Mina and Stephen in each other's arms, inside each other's bodies, their mouths joined, fingers hooked, limbs tangled, sweating torsos aligned; Stephen watching Mina's face buckle as she comes, as he makes her come, as he gives her pleasure. And Mina watching Stephen, feeling Stephen as he comes, hearing him call her name, feeling him right there – all the fractured things become one. Stephen feels as though Mina touches his soul; Mina feels seized, possessed and occupied by Stephen. This is what she wants, and, of course, this is what she fears.

Their time of peace continued; they signed a treaty after a day-trip to Versailles during a weekend in Paris. Mina took the conciliatory role; she held Stephen's hand and remarked on how handsome he was looking. Later, as they walked across the Seine at four a.m. on their way home from a club, Stephen felt romantic; Mina felt his heart beating as he held her. Anyone would have thought they looked happy and secure but the only certainty about love is that it is not possible for anyone to know what goes on between two people, not possible to tell from the outside who is in love and who is not, who is weak and who is strong.

"When she gets behind closed doors," Mina sang in her best Charlie Rich country twang, "and she lets her hair hang down . . ."

"And she makes me proud that I'm a man," Stephen bellowed.

"Cause no one knows what goes on behind closed doors," they sang together.

After a year during which she could not have seen Mina more than three times, Lucy began to find her daughter on her doorstep. Mina would take copies of colour travel brochures to show her mother, offers of cheap holidays which they both knew Lucy would not go on and packages full of expensive, pre-cooked food for dinner. There was no obvious reason for this gradual reconciliation; Mina simply began to think of her mother when, previously, she had not.

Mina thought Lucy should go on a holiday – even she could see that her mother needed to have a rest. Mina believed that there was nothing like travel to put bad thoughts out of one's mind – there was nothing like a holiday for a new lease on life. Lucy needed more than a lease, Mina thought, she needed a brand-new freehold.

"Portugal? Oh, I couldn't go there. They don't speak English, do they?"

"You wouldn't have to worry about that if you went to this resort, Mum. The people who work there speak English. And look at that view, isn't it lovely?"

Lucy was surprised by how infrequently she and Mina quarrelled during these visits. She had learned not to ask her daughter too many questions, and, with some subjects, not to ask any at all. She tried hard not to talk about Harry, not to pass comment on the way Mina looked. Sometimes her daughter came by looking almost translucent, her skin like rice paper, her face shadowed and slightly blue. Other times she appeared so hardy and strong Lucy found herself wondering what exactly her daughter did to maintain such a bloom.

"You're looking well," Lucy said tentatively on one such occasion.

"Yes," replied Mina laughing, "Stephen says it makes him feel ill when I look so well. That's a bit mean, don't you think?"

"A bit mean," nodded Lucy. "How is Stephen?" she asked hesitating. "Everything fine between you two?"

"Yes, everything is okay," replied Mina, considering. "Stephen is well. A bit serious, but fine really. He lets me get on with things."

That night Lucy went to bed warm. Mina was so like Harry when she was in a good mood; she could make one feel light and full of grace. She was also like Harry in the way she could turn it on and snap it off, the ray of charm reduced to an hallucination. Lucy felt almost as happy as she had done after Harry's last healthy visits; she realized she was glad she had loved him, even though she knew he had not really loved her back. At least she had had him, however briefly. Among all the lies and half-truths with which Harry had strung her along – Lucy had never taken Harry's words for more than they were actually worth – at least there was one truth, one thing that was real. There was Mina; not a very good daughter, but a daughter nonetheless.

Mina and Stephen are in bed. Stephen has asked to be tied up and Mina has complied. She has tied his feet together and looped the rope around one end of the bed. She has made him spread his arms wide and has tied his hands to the head of the bed. She has put a pillow under his ass and blindfolded him with a t-shirt. Stephen's eyes are closed and Mina is going down on him. Stephen is moaning softly, he is a long way away. His body is floating in warm, soft air.

Mina begins to kiss Stephen's stomach, her lips moving slowly along his torso, up towards his nipples. He can feel her teeth occasionally, they brush against his skin like stinging nettles in the woods. He wants her to bite his nipples and she does, not too hard, softly. Mina is moaning now, she has her hand between her legs. Stephen wants her to fuck him, but she doesn't. She keeps on kissing and nibbling his body, moving upwards towards his face.

Mina feels very excited, too excited. Her fingers are wet. Stephen's erection strains toward her stomach as she hovers over his body. She knows he wants her but she waits, teasing both herself and him. She feels transported, it is almost like an out-of-body experience. Her desire to fuck him is overwhelming. She begins to feel dizzy, short of breath. Stephen melts out of focus and then back in again. Everything goes black.

Stephen opens his eyes as he feels Mina's teeth. She is biting him again but hard this time. Her teeth tear his skin. It hurts but more than that, he is shocked.

"Mina!" Stephen tries to sit up, forgetting he is bound. "Mina, stop, you're hurting me." Stephen can feel Mina's breath is quick and jagged, she is still biting him. "Mina! Jesus Christ, Mina, stop now." He rocks back and forth, wrenching his shoulders, trying to loosen her grip. Still blindfolded, he bends his head as far as he can and sinks his own teeth into the back of her neck. Mina pulls away in pain. "Look," says Stephen angrily, "I know you get carried away but you shouldn't hurt me. You know that."

Mina feels dazed. There is a little blood dripping from red marks on Stephen's shoulder. She can taste his blood on her tongue, down the back of her throat. All she remembers is wanting to fuck him. She is too embarrassed to ask what happened. She rolls the blindfold down his face and begins to untie her lover. She is shaking. "What were you doing? It hurt. Fuck." Stephen touches the marks gingerly, wincing. Mina can still taste his blood.

"I didn't mean to bite you," she says.

"Ow. What the fuck were you doing?"

"I'm sorry." Mina says, turning her face away. Mina feels ill. She swallows hard. The blood. She feels like a child who's been caught doing something bad. She begins to cry. Stephen pulls a tissue from a box and dabs at his skin, then takes Mina's face in his hands and wipes the tears from her eyes. Still sobbing, Mina begins to move away. Her breasts brush against his chest as she reaches to untie his hands. The sight of her arms – the blue veins so visible – reminds Stephen of the erection he has not lost. He lies very still until she is finished and then, sitting up and pulling himself towards his feet which are still bound, he grabs her and makes her sit on his knees so he can lick her between her legs while he fumbles for a condom. She leans back and then, later, he lets her body slide down his legs until they connect and are inside each other again.

When he comes Stephen begins to cry. He is crying because he is frightened of losing Mina, of losing himself. "It's so scary," he whispers as she strokes his hair. He huddles with his head on her abdomen. His tears run down her body in silver streaks. They drip between her legs and mingle with all the other fluids which are painted on her skin.

Like a normal couple – girl-meets-boy , boy's-parents-do-not-lose-son-but-gain-daughter – Mina and Stephen began to visit Ben and Anna together. Mina liked going to the Smith's house – she liked to sit at the kitchen table with Anna and her books while Stephen and Ben talked elsewhere. She and Anna would have conversations about travel and psychology.

"I'll never understand all the Freudian fuss about families," Mina said one day. "I'm a bastard," – Anna tried not to flinch at the word – "so I never had a father to be, well, strange with but I don't think I'm any better or worse off than anyone else. It's just different. I also don't understand," she continued, "all the business about analysis. Surely talking about your fears only transforms them into something else – I don't believe fear itself can ever really go away."

Anna laughed and said "You're probably right." Then she attempted to explain to Mina what she found interesting about the texts. Mina's point of view was always intriguing but for some reason, which Anna could not bring herself to analyse, her basic distrust of her younger son's girlfriend would not go away.

Stephen did not enjoy spending time with Ben when Mina was around; he found it difficult to listen to his father while trying to hear what was going on in the kitchen. His father always seemed to want to talk about work – how much Stephen was making for a living, what his plans were, "expansion". It was never very long before Stephen would say he was hungry and wander back into the kitchen, his father – still talking – behind him.

Despite their current domestic tranquillity, Stephen was not surprised to learn that Mina did not want him to move in with her. "It will be cheaper," he tried arguing, somewhat cheaply. "It will be cosy. I won't worry so much."

"You'll be able to keep an eye on me."

"No! I'll be able to cook you dinner on Sundays."

"I didn't like living with Lucy and I don't see why

living with you should be that much different."

Stephen was mortified by the comparison. He changed the subject. "So, can you come away with me on my next trip?"

"I can't take another holiday for some time." Mina was cross. She felt Stephen was nagging. "I'm going away next week to a conference anyway. Portuguese Tourist Initiatives. I'll be gone until Saturday."

While Mina was away Stephen dreamed of broken promises. When he woke he realized he could not force Mina to promise anything. Things change, people change, "I love you" cannot mean "I'll always love you" however much one wishes it would. Stephen felt a rising desperation.

In a luxury hotel on the Algarve – "sufficient" was what she would write in her report – Mina was in the bath shaving her legs. She hummed as she ran a disposable razor meant for a man's face up one side of her calf. She liked the labour-intensiveness of this ritual, so different from the easy convenience of chemical hair-removers. Mina loved the way the line of Stephen's jaw re-emerged as he used the razor. Shaving her legs had a cleansing effect upon her: lots of hot water, the razorblade and the pleasure of touching herself.

Stephen had shaved her legs for her once. While she lay back in the bath, one leg lifted to its rim, Stephen had held her calf in his hand as he moved the razor carefully. Mina had never cut herself whilst shaving;

her procedure was too fetishistic for that, having as much to do with relaxation as with smooth legs. But today she was in a hurry. She was getting ready to go to a meeting and did not have quite enough time. The steam from the bath clouded her vision momentarily – there, she did it, sliced through the skin just above her ankle.

Mina stared at the white gash for a moment. Could she see bone, was this what she looked like inside? Then the blood came and as it built up Mina began to hear her pulse pounding deep inside her brain. When the blood began to run Mina felt she needed to stop herself from spilling out but as she leaned forward everything went dark.

Stephen woke in the middle of the night; he knew something had happened to Mina. He got up and dialled the number where she was staying – the concierge put the call through to Mina's room. There was no answer, not even after thirty rings.

At first he felt fear but then that gradually reddened into jealousy. Stephen felt that somehow he was being betrayed.

Mina has to get out. She needs to get out into the fresh air. She needs to get out there and fill her lungs. She needs to feel her heart pound, her pulse race, she needs . . . she does not stop to think about what it is.

When she awoke Mina was lying on the floor of the

bathroom. The room was dark. A little light shone in through the window which, when she looked up, Mina saw had been smashed and left glass-free. As she began to move she felt bits of glass on the floor where she put her hands. She stood and turned on the light.

There was blood dripping from the window, running slowly down the side of the over-full tub. The mirror, the towels on the rack, the walls, the tiles: everything was smeared unevenly. And her body, it was as though she had been coated in blood, dipped in it by some barbaric confectioner.

Slowly Mina began to wash down the walls and floor, scrubbing harder as, gradually, she came fully awake. Stopping up the door with a once-white red towel, she threw water over everything. She used her hairbrush in the places where the blood had begun to harden and coagulate. And then she started on herself.

In the mirror Mina's face looked strange, a vision of herself as corpse. Red rimmed eyes, blood-washed skin, nostrils caked with it, mouth sticky. She filled the sink but soon gave up and got into the bath with the shower-head, watching the blood stream away. She was covered in cuts, and the original slash on her ankle had deepened and spread as though her skin had begun to peel back. But worse was the smell. Mina did not recognize the smell of blood on her skin; it was different from the smell which still seeped from her ankle and some of the other tiny wounds. The red water swirled down the drain in the bath, the blood washed out of sight. Mina rinsed her hair last of all.

Then she walked towards the bed. The clock said 0300. There was nothing on TV.

Mina cannot explain what has happened – she has no memory of these events, not even a dream of a memory. It is as though she forgets the minute the blood disappears down the drain. How could she live with remembering?

Travelling back from the conference Mina's flight was delayed. She had said she would go straight to Stephen's flat. He was waiting for her. He paced the sitting room, back and forth, back and forth, his hands covering his ears from time to time as he hunched and relaxed his shoulders. He had never felt so jealous; he had believed he was beyond jealousy, that he could deal with whatever Mina did. But now faced with something new after she had made her promise, Stephen had never been so angry.

Stephen does not want to lose Mina. For a long time she has helped him to define himself and he does not like the thought of a world without her. Before Mina walks through the door he has lost and won her back a hundred times over.

Finally Stephen heard Mina's knock at the door. He felt his spine stiffen as he attempted to look relaxed. She used her key as he sat on the sofa and pretended to watch a late-night film. Mina placed her suitcases in the corridor, Stephen heard her sniff and sigh, run her hands through her hair. He knew these movements too well.

Mina walked by the sitting room, glancing through the door. She stopped and turned around. She looked healthy and relaxed.

"Hello Stephen, my flight was delayed."

"Yes?" Stephen answered. He could feel anger rising in his gut.

"It was chaos at the airport and then it took ages for our bags to come through."

"Yes?" said Stephen, standing, barely in control. He wanted to fling himself at her, take hold of her thin shoulders and shake her until she confessed.

"I need a cup of tea," she said, starting towards his kitchen.

"Mina!" Stephen shouted, "you bitch." He lowered his voice. "What happened last night? What have you been doing? You're a fucking slut, aren't you?"

Mina stopped at the doorway of the sitting room. She turned slowly. "What did you call me?"

"It's true then, isn't it? I know what's going on." Stephen's face was red, his eyes brimming. He had his hands clenched, his lips pulled tight together, his jaw so taut he could barely speak.

Mina thought Stephen looked vulnerable, like a child afraid of being hurt, waiting for its parents' wrath to descend. She took a few steps toward him.

"Don't come near me!" Stephen shouted. He sat back down, drawing his legs up so he could clutch his knees. Mina kept advancing, her arms loose at her sides. She was amazed by Stephen's display of pain. It was as though he had been knifed. She had not told him anything about her trip; what was it that he knew she had done? Mina dropped down onto the edge of the settee right beside where Stephen sat curled and shaking. She put her hand out and touched his arm. He wrenched himself free and shouted his question: "Have you been with someone else?"

Mina's mouth went dry. She looked up at the ceiling, her eyes scraping against their lids. What have I done, she wondered for the first time. What happened last night?

Stephen's legs shot out, he held his body rigid as he stood. He hurled himself across the room somehow, away from Mina, slumping against the sitting room door, forcing it shut. He doubled over again, his hands clutching his hair. He slid to the floor and seemed very small. Mina stared. She felt her eyes fill with tears. Stephen was moaning in the corner. She rose and lurched towards him. She wanted to take him in her arms.

"Don't touch me you bitch!" he screamed. "Why? Why did you have to do it? I hate you, you don't ever think about me. You are horrible, you don't love me, you are evil."

"Stephen," she whispered, "I never meant to hurt you."

"Why did you do it then? Of course you fucking meant to hurt me. How else could it make me feel? Happy?" Stephen was still screaming, his voice like electronic feedback, amplified. Mina felt shattered. She knelt on the floor next to the body of her lover. "You are shit, Mina." She reached out a hand and laid it on

Stephen's shoulder. The force with which he recoiled knocked her over. He moved across the room away from her again.

Mina whispered, "What have I done? What did I do? Who do you want me to be, Stephen?"

"Get out," he shouted, "get out. You can't stay here tonight. I don't want you in the same building. Take your suitcases back downstairs. Get out! Take them before I throw them out the window."

Mina stood, straightening her skirt. "I'm on fire," Stephen said, his voice lowered. "I am burning up." Mina ran a hand through her hair. She sniffed at her fingers. They smelt of something slightly muddy, of blood and something else. She looked down at her lover on the floor and felt sorry for him. Then she left the way she came, taking her cases with her. Stephen balled up his body even smaller. He was weeping. All he could think was that he hated her and he wished she hadn't left.

Mina sits in front of the mirror. Her face seems to be drooping. There is nothing there for her to admire, nothing about the image that she likes. She bites her lips to make them redder. She looks so pale. Reaching for the tweezers, she raises one eyebrow before beginning to pluck. The hairs seem to be getting thicker. All the hair on her body seems to grow faster as she gets older, like weeds on a compost heap.

In love, there are things remembered and things that are

forgotten. Who can remember what love was like before a new laove came by? Mina says to Stephen who is not there to hear, "You never loved anyone before you loved me." Then she says, "I'll never love anyone like I love you." She knows these are the best kind of lies.

*

Like Mina, Lucy conquered her fear of loneliness through work. She appeared to believe that labour was the best medicine as though she had been brought up by evangelical presbyterians or some other kind of protestant fanatic. In fact she did not believe in the healing power of work; it was merely the most readily available way of stuffing full all the gaping holes in her life.

The young, male manager whose appointment Mina had objected to eventually moved on to greater things and Lucy found herself applying for his job. She got Mina to help her with a letter to Personnel. Much to both of their surprise a month later she was promoted. Mina took her mother out to celebrate.

"So how is Stephen?" Lucy asked.

Mina frowned. Although she and her mother were getting on better she was not prepared to tell her that Stephen had thrown her out. Ever since it happened Mina had worked hard to keep that night – and Stephen's accusations – out of her mind. This was proving to be difficult.

"How is your flat?" Lucy tried again.

"It's all right."

"I'd like to come and see the new table."

"Uh-huh, you'll have to do that."

"Any trips planned?"

Mina took a sip from her drink and relaxed a little as she explained to Lucy the ins and outs of what she was currently doing for the company. "They are giving me a car next month."

"You can't drive!"

"They're giving me lessons as well."

"Why?"

"It's a perk." If holidays were like a drug then Mina was a dealer. "Listen mum, I can get you a free trip to a really wonderful resort on the Mediterranean." Lucy had still never been abroad despite Mina's many offers. "All you have to do is tell me whether or not you like the place once you've been there. You must have about ten years worth of holidays saved up."

After another couple of drinks Mina had her mother almost convinced. "You're so persuasive," Lucy said smiling, "you make it sound like such a good idea."

"Well, you are the ultimate sales challenge. I'd be admitting failure if I couldn't sell my own mother a holiday."

On the way home Lucy began to like the idea and by the end of that week she was excited: a promotion and a holiday, these are things that go together in life. She rang Mina. "I'm keen now," she said. "How soon can I go?"

Lucy's decision cheered Mina a little – it made her feel she could do something right. At least there was one relationship she was capable of salvaging. Since Stephen had thrown her out she had felt numb. She kept seeing his face mutilated by pain; she kept waking in the night and reaching out to touch him. She tried to steady herself by wearing more make-up, tighter dresses with lower necklines and shoes with higher heels. She had her hair cut differently; she wore a new scent. The men in the office became even more obsequious than usual, scampering around her desk like bunny rabbits, begging her to pounce.

Stephen lay awake and fantaized that Mina was about to climb in through the window, get into his bed and take his unsuspecting body in her arms. He had not seen Mina for weeks, not since the night he threw her out; he was leaving soon for a long trip through Canada.

Stephen's fantasy goes like this: Mina climbs in through the window. She is dressed in a black bodysuit, like a cat-burglar in an American movie from the 1950s, except she has on extremely high heels. Stephen is asleep, naked. He does not hear Mina when she enters the room. She walks over to the bed and folds the bedclothes away from his body. Lying on his side facing away, still he does not waken. Without taking her clothes off Mina lies down beside him. She begins to run her hands up and down his body, gently, barely touching him. Stephen continues to sleep. His cock begins to harden. Mina touches his nipples then arches her body over his to lick them. She is growling, Stephen's breath is heavy with sleep. Lying beside him again, she places her hand on his cock and begins to move it up and down. She sticks her finger into her mouth and then, not so gently, slides it into Stephen's asshole.

Stephen wakes suddenly. For a moment he thinks he is being raped by a stranger but then he realizes it is Mina. She is masturbating him with one hand, fucking his arse with the other. He attempts to struggle but before he can stop her Mina has wriggled out of her bodysuit, pushed Stephen onto his back and pinned him down. Before he knows what is happening she has got on top of him and they struggle hard. Stephen sits up while still inside Mina and attempts to push her over but can't; she has him pinned down and she is fucking him, she is moving her hips in a quick rhythm, clenching her teeth with pleasure. But before Stephen can get to this moment in his fantasy he feels himself begin to come and he can not stop as he moves his own hand up and down his cock, harder and faster, until it is too late.

Stephen curls his body into a very tight ball, tears squeeze from his screwed-tight eyes as he wishes for precisely the hundredth time that he had never met Mina, never caught sight of her at all.

Before leaving for Canada Stephen went to visit Ben and Anna. His visits had not been as regular of late and so he was prepared for the inevitable questions.

"How is Mina?"

"I don't know."

"What is it that you do to that poor girl?"

"I don't *do* anything to her."

"Maybe that's the problem then."

"She is hardly a girl anyway." Stephen was always surprised by his father's ability to make him feel fourteen again. Anna came into the room.

"How are you Stephen?" she asked.

"Okay."

"Off tomorrow then? You'll remember to look up your cousin Rachel when you are in Montreal? I would love some photographs of her and her children."

"Rachel has children?" Stephen felt momentarily guilty.

"Yes, I told you that."

"Oh."

"How is Mina?"

"Don't ask," Ben interrupted. "You'll only get a series of abrupt, ugly noises in reply." Anna looked surprised.

"I've sort of, well, called the whole thing to a halt," Stephen said by way of explanation. As usual, his parents had managed to pinpoint his most vulnerable spot with military precision, turning the full glare of their floodlights upon him.

"You mean she has dumped you?" asked Ben. Anna gave her husband a warning glance then turned to see how Stephen would respond.

"No. I dumped her. And I don't want to talk about it."

"Why not Stephen?" asked Anna. "Sometimes it is good to discuss these things."

"Maybe if I felt in need of analysis it would be good to discuss it, but I don't. You are my parents and I don't want to talk about it."

"That's our son," said Ben, "always frank, no matter how rude that might be."

"Listen, I'm sorry if you find me impolite but really, the only reason I ever come to visit is because of the food so where are the cakes and let's talk about something else."

Stephen walked into the kitchen, his parents trailing after him. "Seen any good plays lately Dad?"

The next day Stephen flew to Vancouver. The blandness of the city coincided with the blank hardness Stephen felt within himself. There was nothing in Canada to remind him of Mina except his very self. Before this trip Stephen had always travelled to get away from wanting Mina; this time he travelled to get away from Mina wanting him.

In London Mina embarked on a cycle of sleeplessness which left her feeling more tired than ever before, a new, insidious kind of fatigue. She began to have the same dream night after night. In this dream she came home from work, opened the door of her flat, and was nearly overwhelmed by the smell. Somewhere something large was rotting. She went straight into the kitchen and stood staring at her cupboards. What had she forgotten to throw away? Had she emptied the rubbish recently?

After a brief search Mina realized that the smell must be coming from somewhere else so she left the kitchen and wandered into the sitting room, following her nose and trying not to gag. The dining table sat next to the glass doors which led to the garden. On top of the table, which Mina had polished twice over the weekend as if expecting company, were the remains of Harry.

The body was stretched out on its back facing the ceiling. It was at a fairly advanced stage of decomposition, although hardly as advanced as it should have been for someone who had been dead for such a long time. Barely in one piece, the body looked bloated and its skin was tinged with green. Abdominal gas had compressed Harry's lungs and forced blood into his mouth; this ran down one side of his face as though he was a hospital patient forced to drink while lying down. His eyes were open and bloodshot, his nails had grown long and his clothes were filthy and torn. Mina even thought she could see the ominous beginnings of an erection.

In her nightmare, she spoke to him politely in an attempt to disguise her terror. "Harry! I wasn't expecting you. How are you and why am I honoured with this visit?" Harry did not reply. Mina stepped closer to the table. She leaned over the corpse and looked down at his eyes. He was dead all right. She poked him in the arm and he did not flinch although she thought she heard the faint sound of gas escaping from somewhere. "How revolting," Mina said, straightening. "You are not the man you used to be." Suddenly Harry's dead face became animated. He bared his teeth in a grimace, his lips cracking and splitting as he turned his head to look at Mina. He sat up, stretched out his arms and said, "I love you, Mina, be mine."

Night after night Mina woke with a shout. Despite her dread, she would get up and force herself to go look in her sitting room which, as always, was empty. But each night she thought she could smell a strange odour hanging in the air. It smelt like corruption, like some kind of sin. Throwing open the doors and windows

Mina would frantically wave her arms to try to get rid of it. In the shower she would scrub hard to get the smell off her skin. Then she would sit and wait until it was time to go to work. She listened to the radio and watched breakfast TV, trying not to think.

The list of things Mina does not want to think about is growing longer. But, whatever else is on this list, at the top is always Stephen, his body, and his face.

Stephen, his body, his face.

At work when Lucy announced she was going away for a holiday her colleagues were all very surprised and this added to her pleasure. She was encouraged to go as soon as possible. She rang Mina every day.

"Yes, and it's all fine with the head office and Margaret can do my job for me while I'm away and they said they were going to give me a bon voyage party but I don't think that is such a good idea, I mean for heaven's sake, I will only be gone for a week and other people go off for much longer or leave for good and they don't get parties given to them. But if we do go out for drinks the night before I would like for you to come, the girls would like to see you, it's been quite a while since you have been in . . ."

Mina had never heard Lucy talk like this before and, despite her own depression, found herself getting excited about her mother's plans. Lucy was hungry for advice, mouthfuls and mouthfuls of advice, on what to take, what to wear at different times during the day, what people did to amuse themselves in the resort, if she should take her own towels, whether she would be able to eat the food, how hot it would be, etc. Mina felt something had been unleashed.

"Next thing you'll be wanting me to get you a cheap flight to Kenya and you'll be off with all my yuppies."

"Oh, I don't know about Kenya," said Lucy, "but someone in the office has been where I'm going and she says it's very nice."

At the airport Mina took her mother into the bar for a calming drink. Lucy had on a sun hat and was carrying a bright red beach bag. She was very excited and seemed quite unafraid; it was Mina who was worried now.

"Don't be too friendly to strange men, you know mum, sometimes they hang out at the nicer resorts looking for ladies like you to rip off."

"Nobody is going to rip off me."

"And don't spend too long in the sun at first." Mina was almost put out by her mother's confidence; she had expected to have to push her onto the plane. During the past week she had hardly slept from the cocktail of worry and nightmares. And that smell was still there every morning, lingering like a stain. She had great dark rings under her eyes and was looking too thin. That morning she had woken with Stephen's name on her lips. Where was he?

"How will I know when it is time to board my plane?" Lucy was saying. "Mina?"

Mina turned and looked at her mother. Stephen had gone and now Lucy was going away too. She took a sip of her drink. They had ordered doubles. "Stephen's left me," she said, regretting it immediately.

But Lucy was looking the other way and without turning said, "When will he be back? How am I going to tell when it's time to board my plane?"

Mina waved goodbye as Lucy disappeared into the departure lounge. It was late by the time she got back to her flat. She had a bath and then, with her body and her head wrapped in towels, walked into her bedroom. Every window in the flat was open in an effort to clear the smell. Little spring breezes lifted the pages of newspapers and magazines. Mina dropped the towels and lay on her bed. She moved her hands down along her body. Quickly and silently she made herself come while thinking about Stephen. Afterwards she whispered his name, once, twice, three times.

Stephen was now in Calgary, far, far away from Mina's moans. He felt that Canada had been the right choice – here he could make the space he had put between Mina and himself tangible. Things seemed separate and clear in Canada: places were far apart. On the prairie especially, flat and empty – if she was to come after him he would see her, like a dust storm on the highway, while she was still hundreds of miles away.

That night in London the breeze turned into a strong

gale. The wind lifted the covers off Mina's bed and dropped them back into place then lifted and dropped and lifted and dropped them again. Mina was not in the flat. She had been there but now she was gone. The rooms smelt as clean and fresh as rooms ever do in London.

By dawn Mina was asleep under her troubled bedclothes. The windows were all still wide open but the smell, dark, putrefied and slightly perfumed, had come back as well. She woke in the early morning light with a trench-warfare headache, her back hurting, her mouth fuzzy and sour as though she had drunk a lot.

This giant fatigue was beginning to make her falter at work. The purposeful forgetfulness she maintained in some parts of her life was starting to spill over into others. She forgot where she parked the car, she forgot where she put things, important files, information. She forgot the names of colleagues. One morning she forgot to shower. As soon as she sat down at her desk she realized that Harry, or rather, Harry's smell, had followed her to the office. Mina rushed to the toilet and vomited blood.

On a Friday night while Stephen was still away Mina was invited to a party by a colleague. She dressed up, determined to feel good. Once there she looked around the room for a man who showed something she could recognize. She spotted him standing in a corner; he was unoccupied. Walking towards him, Mina tried to feel strong. He would notice her breasts first, she thought; she could feel his hands on her body already.

The man ignored her. Mina turned away, suddenly very angry.

Desire is a fleeting, briefly glimpsed, burning thing: something there and then something gone. With strange men Mina could renew herself over and over – they made her feel desired: then, being desired was enough. She always wants the one who wants her the most: it is only now she realizes this is Stephen.

Stephen missed Mina's revelation; he was in the middle of a snowstorm in Winnipeg, Manitoba. When entering the city he had seen a sign that read "WELCOME TO WINNIPEG, THE COLDEST CITY IN THE WORLD".

"Besides," he said aloud to no one in particular, "she never actually said she loved me anyway."

Mina feels tricked by Stephen, by Harry, by the world, by herself. She continues to dream about Harry's decaying body but now she rails at it. "I thought the thing was to be independent, but it's not, is it? Why can't I be loved without having to give in?"

Her bed is empty most nights.

Lucy came back from her holiday with a tan and a boyfriend. Mina was as shocked as her mother had been the day she found Mina's birth control pills.

They met at the airport. When the man kissed Lucy goodbye Mina stared.

"What's the matter?" hissed Lucy after he had gone. "You look like you've never seen anyone kiss me before."

"I haven't."

"Now don't be difficult Mina. How's Stephen?"

"We're not seeing each other at this moment in time."

Lucy clicked her tongue and shook her head. "You are as bad as Harry was, you know that?"

"Have you slept with that man?"

Lucy stopped walking and looked at her daughter.

"Do you let him fuck you, do you give yourself to him?"

Lucy's face moved from shock to another place completely.

"Does he love you?" Mina asked bitterly. Lucy thought it was as though Harry himself was speaking. She found herself wordless, silenced again.

In her flat at dawn, without having slept, Mina stands alone in front of the mirror and sees nothing reflected back. Without Stephen to remind her of who she is there is nothing. She is composed of other people's perceptions; she relies on being reflected upon. No one she knows would suspect that she could find herself dependent on one man. As she stands there Mina thinks she can actually feel her body aging. She needs Stephen in order to survive; he counteracts the darker forces in her life.

*

When he returned from Canada Stephen did not ring Mina. He barely managed one desultory phone call to his parents.

"Did you see your cousin Rachel?" Ben asked.

"Did you see her babies?" asked Anna on the other phone.

"Did you take pictures?" they asked simultaneously.

"No, no, no," said Stephen.

"Well, at least we know he's alive," Anna said after they had hung up.

"I'm glad he's alive," said Ben, "so I can wring his neck next time we see him."

Since arriving back Stephen was having trouble getting down to work. He did not feel like going anywhere else, he had no curiosity about anything except his own moods. Writing seemed too difficult; he had had an okay time in Canada but, once home, it immediately seemed as though he had never been away. Travel seemed like a trivial activity; travel writing even more so. Why go to places where culture can only be viewed from the outside, without real understanding or experience? Why float around the world examining the way things appear, recording impressions, details of impressions, word-pictures and nothing else? What good could it possibly do for anyone, including himself?

For Stephen these questions remained unanswered. Sometimes they bothered him more, sometimes less.

Mina was still having bad nights. She would wake in the morning covered with bruises. At work early, she would attack her desk, sloppy with false energy and haste. She stayed late at the office, telling herself and Lucy that she was not interested in anything else. "There is nothing as satisfying as working hard, long and well," she claimed even though these days she often sat at her desk and did nothing for hours on end.

But work had suddenly become quite unimportant to Lucy – she reacted to Mina with scepticism. She kept ringing her daughter despite the things Mina had said to her. Somehow she knew that something else lay behind those words, something else apart from jealousy and loss. She knew it was not simply that Mina hated to see her mother happy, not simply part of the way the girl had always protected Harry.

"She's pining," she said to her boyfriend after she had taken Mina out for lunch one day. "I know she is, she is not a happy girl."

"She looks well enough to me."

"She looks well, yes, but Mina always looks her best when she is unhappiest. It's just one of those things; some people never look more lovely than when they are ill."

Lucy's boyfriend took her to the cinema, he bought her flowers, they cooked together. They behaved liked courting teenagers and were not cautious, they were not careful. They smooched on the up escalator in the underground. In all of London it seemed no one was in love like them. Seeing them together made Mina feel sick.

"Do you have to be so fucking girlish?" she asked.

"Do you have to hold hands all the time?" Lucy smiled benignly and ignored what her daughter said.

Mina is accustomed to being alone; it is the way she usually feels. Lucy also thinks of herself as solitary. Both women are shocked by their new circumstances – for the first time ever Mina is lonely while Lucy is not.

At home by himself Stephen listened to the same records over and over but even his old favourites did not make him feel any better.

Mina sat on the edge of her bed thinking about Stephen. "Come back," she thought again and again until she finally began to say it out loud. "Come back," she said, more and more loudly, "come back to me Stephen. You are mine."

Time went by very slowly. Each day that passed nudged Stephen toward Mina. He could not hang on much longer. Mina wanted him back. And he could not maintain his resistance, especially now that he was in London; he was too lonely, she knew him too well. Stephen's body ached. He knew it was Mina who would dull that ache, smother it and make it go away.

Even from afar Mina was a force, drawing him toward her, like a siren. It was as though he could hear her beckoning to him through the night. Sometimes in the morning he could swear that she had actually been there with him. Stephen felt powerless. He began to doubt his decision. What could he possibly lose by going back to her? What was the point of being unhappy without her when he could be unhappy with her? At least then the sex would be real. It would be so easy to go back to her; it would be simple for him to decide he was stupid not to. No one would blame him, apart from himself.

One day Mina knocked on Stephen's door. He knew it was her before opening it. "Come back to me," was all she said. Stephen stood to one side as she walked in.

The thing about being back together again was that it seemed so precious and fragile, like a croupy baby's still moments.

Mina made Stephen a new set of promises. She presented them to him as she would a birthday gift.

"I promise," she said, "to stay with you. I promise not to leave you. I promise to be faithful. I promise to want you – only you – always. I promise to need only you."

They were lying in bed. All Stephen could manage was a nod. He believed her this time. He believed every word she said.

And Mina believes every word she says to Stephen. She does want to be with him; she does want them to be one; she recognizes that she needs this. It is not fidelity that she wants, it is not monogamy: it is Stephen. She wants Stephen. Nothing else.

But Mina is not Mina alone, no. She has Harry and Hilda standing behind her and they watch her now, they watch her always. Mina needs something that neither Stephen nor Mina herself understand or recognize. Mina should fear the night, she should fear what she becomes. But she does not.

Despite the fact that Stephen and Mina were sleeping together almost every night – some nights at his flat, others at hers, sitting up in bed talking, exhausting each other with conversation and then the painful reconstruction of sex – Stephen was still not sleeping well. He would fall like a dead body into slumber but was soon disturbed by dreams, streaming nightmares about his childhood, his friends, episodes from daily life turned upside-down. He began to put on weight, his skin took on a kind of flabby slackness. He became lazy and continually sleepy.

One night he woke in the dark. A strange tingling sensation – he had felt it before, he knew that much – began at his head and travelled down his body to his feet. Then it passed away. He turned over but Mina was not there. He fell back asleep.

In the morning he woke with Mina beside him. She turned toward him and kissed his drowsy lips, one hand placed on his hip. They made love sleepily. Stephen did not remember to ask if Mina had been up during the night.

This happened every night and every morning for a while. Stephen grew weaker. The tingling sensation intensified; it would happen once, twice, three times in the same night. After Mina had left for work Stephen would lie in the bath for an hour, fiddling with the taps to keep the water hot. He drank lots of coffee and sat at his desk, going through his notebooks, thinking about the past. He had Mina back now, that was all he wanted. There was no reason for him to feel so bad.

One day Ben dropped by. Stephen took a long time to answer his knock, crossing the room to get his dressing gown, turning off his computer, and then finally shuffling over to the door. He opened it and stood stooping like an old man.

"Oh, it's you," he said just about managing a smile. "Hello, come in."

"Yes, it's me. Your mother and I were wondering if you had forgotten about us."

"Why aren't you at work?"

"Work is not the only thing there is in life, you know."

Stephen frowned at his father and offered him a cup of coffee. The flat smelt awful, like there was something rotting in it. "Given up on getting dressed then?" said Ben.

"No, I just haven't been feeling all that well lately."

"What you need is a wife."

"Mina is not very good at housework and that kind of thing, in fact, I'm much more domestic than her."

"Mina?" said Ben, raising his eyebrows. Stephen nodded without looking at his father. "Well, despite your true love having reappeared, you do not look very good on it."

"My true love," Stephen repeated. "My true love."

"And how is she?"

"Very well. Working hard. Thriving."

"While you moulder away in your flat. I suggest you get yourself together Stephen or she'll be walking out again before you know it."

"My life sounds so dramatic when you talk about it."

"Well, your mother is fine, in case you are interested."

"And my brother?"

"More successful every day."

"And you?"

"Me? I've gone into semi-retirement. I'm thinking about learning to play golf."

"Golf. You'll have to wear those awful golfer clothes and shoes."

"Are you eating enough?" Ben asked abruptly. "Are you getting enough sleep? You haven't started taking drugs or anything? I thought we were past the dangerous age with you – you are practically thirty, after all."

"I am not practically thirty."

"Well, you might as well be. I'm old enough for my youngest son to be thirty. I'm old enough to play golf." Ben made Stephen get dressed and then took him out to lunch.

Every morning after making love to Stephen Mina would shower, dress carefully and make her way to work feeling strong and confident. Being with Stephen every night made her feel more like other people, something she had never thought she might like. Being with only Stephen – Stephen for breakfast, Stephen for dinner, Stephen for a bedtime snack – made Mina feel desired in a steady way; she concentrated everything in his direction. She began to go to the gym to work out regularly, amazed by how quickly she became much stronger.

The biggest surprise for Mina was that Stephen had not gone off her yet. Part of her waited for this to happen. Part of her waited for the boredom to set in, for either one of them to walk out. She was not much of a nurse – as he weakened she tried to compensate by bringing him more and more expensive take-away food. The urge to feed Stephen was not a maternal one, it was just that Mina could think of nothing else to do. And despite his lack of energy they still gave each other great pleasure. In fact as Stephen got worse, sex got better – it was the one thing he still had energy for. Apart from feeding him Mina ignored what was happening to her lover. She did not have time to wonder what was causing his slump; it was not within the range of her vision.

Stephen could be relied upon and that felt very new and strange to Mina. He told her she was beautiful and she believed him. She imagined that this was what it would be like if they lived together, if they were married. Stephen would be there without her having to think about him, like part of the furniture, like a nice old settee. That did not alarm her now.

Mina felt more on top of things than usual. She knew she was obsessed with control but even though it was something she worked hard at, devoted time and money to, it was still something she felt she failed to achieve. Ordinarily she felt out of control, on the edge, on the verge of panic. For the first time being with Stephen regularly was not claustrophobic. All she wanted was him, nothing else. She slept better, she did not dream, she did not have dizzy spells, she had not had a blackout since they got back together. Other men no longer seemed interesting. She was convinced Stephen could give her everything she needed. She could not explain this change. It just happened like things do – that was then, this is now. She felt happy, she felt strong, she felt content. Stephen slumped further and further, even forgetting to feel guilty about not working. Even as a student, sloth was a luxury he had never allowed himself. Now, he thought grimly, he aspired to sloth on a good day.

Stephen had not felt he could be destroyed by love, in fact he had believed the opposite. But it was not love that was destroying him.

"I'm yours," Mina said.

"Mine?"

"Yours," she said. They were fucking.

Stephen closed his eyes. "Mine."

"Fuck me."

"Mine."

"Come on Stephen, I want you. Come on." Mina wanted to be fucked harder. She wanted him to prove his desire again. Stephen pulled his shirt off and put it across her mouth. He pinned her down with it, one hand on either side of her head. He moved his hips quickly, arching his back so he could look at himself, at the point where their bodies met. It felt incredible, it always did. It felt new, It always felt different. He moved faster – he wanted her to come.

And when she came she shouted, grabbing Stephen's ass, feeling faint. Stephen also came, pushing himself as far inside her as he could. He fell forward onto her and stayed lying there, her body between him and the bed, falling asleep right away. In his sleep Mina dissolved before him. She spread out into the air like an image on film, as though she had been a sculpture made from flour.

Stephen staggered out of bed. "Mina?" He wandered around naked calling her name, but the flat was small and he had known immediately that she was not there. It occurred to him that perhaps she had left him but he doubted that, it would be too unexpected this time. He wandered back into the bedroom.

There was a strong smell of dirt, freshly churned up sour mud, and a kind of glow in the room. It was as if a layer of dust had been stirred and lit by a ray of sunshine or an exceptionally bright moon. Stephen thought for a moment he saw Mina standing behind the curtain – but no, it was just a shadow. He stepped forward and climbed onto the bed. He stood, his feet buried in the disarray of bedclothes, bouncing slightly as the mattress moved beneath his weight. He could smell Mina's perfume – that was it, that was what was so familiar about the smell. It was as though Mina had come back into the room.

And where is Mina, Stephen wonders later. And where has Mina been? Is she the same person as the one Stephen thinks he loves? People – lovers – must continually realign their perspectives in order to carry on seeing the same thing, in order to remain within each other's sights.

Where is she, he wonders. Where has she been?

Lucy had been left bankrupt by both Harry and Mina once upon a time. Harry had been her master and she had been his slave. He forced himself inside her and then blackmailed her with pleasure for the rest of his life. It happens all the time, this thing called love. Except Harry died and Mina grew up and Lucy made her escape. People are betrayed by their children, their lovers, their parents but, now, Lucy felt she had finally stopped betraying herself. And this new love, this new man – no matter how long it lasted – made Lucy feel as if life was not about to run away from her again.

Stephen has always worried about death. When he was a child he worried that his parents might die, now it is Mina. He dreams at night of his own death and he fears that as well.

Mina does not fear death, it is something she faces. She can see it; it has bloody hands and a bloody face.

One evening that week Stephen saw something out of the corner of his eye. He was in Mina's flat in front of the television. It was late, Mina was asleep but Stephen had slept most of the afternoon and, consequently, was wide awake. He hated not being able to sleep; it made him feel lonely, even with Mina in the next room.

The door to Mina's bedroom was ajar, Stephen had his back to it. He was looking straight ahead at the television screen, not really watching but staring. Stephen felt maudlin and sorry for himself. Then something moved behind him. Had Mina got out of bed? Stephen turned his head. There was nothing. He went back into his torpor. During a commercial, it happened again. He saw something move out of the corner of his eye, to the right. A little flash of light perhaps, a tiny flinch, a blink. Stephen turned fully around, stretching out of the chair. Of course there was nothing. A wave of fatigue passed through him – he stood and began to walk toward the bedroom.

It happens then. He is not expecting it. It takes him by surprise.

Sometimes Mina wonders just before she forgets: what have I done? What am I doing?

A week later Stephen was still in the hospital.

The doctors told him he was anaemic and suffering a kind of long term blood deficiency – he simply did not have enough blood. No one could explain this. They said Mina had found him unconscious; he had almost died. The doctors could not explain this either but they seemed to have given up trying to explain much of anything. The consultant who was looking after Stephen's case felt he had seen too many strange things happen in the operating theatre to maintain empirical faith – "theatre is the operative word" was the medical witticism he was currently bandying about the wards.

The hospital seemed a sickly microcosm of the world to Stephen. From the mortuary to the barber shop, life and death went on. The nurses pumped him full of other people's blood: he felt obliged to be fresh with them.

Mina visited Stephen every evening, sitting beside his bed holding his hand. Sometimes if he had been given an injection she seemed extraordinarily ethereal and far away. Other times her face loomed large above him bringing back memories of when he had been ill as a child and his mother's worried face had hovered beside the bedside lamp.

The hospital gave Mina the creeps. She remembered visiting Harry and, before him, Hilda; by all appearances the occupants of the surrounding beds had not changed. Every day part of her expected Stephen to be dead when she arrived. When he was not she felt pleased and intimidated.

Ben and Anna visited in the afternoons bearing armful of gifts – food, flowers, books, games. Ben wanted to play draughts but Stephen felt his father saw himself as a character in some obscure melodrama and did not feel up to playing along.

Stephen had begun to feel better very quickly once he woke up and realized he was in the hospital. Here were people who confirmed his fears while soothing him at the same time. He was ill, but he would get better. His body sucked up the donated, tested and screened blood like a leech.

Mina does not remember what happened to Stephen the night he collapsed. All she remembers is suddenly finding him lying on the floor at her feet. She remembers he looked washed out, not quite there, as though only pausing on the way to another place. She does not wonder how he got there, she does not consider her role in all this. She loves him, isn't that enough?

The night before Stephen is due to be released he dreams that he is sitting in his bed surveying the dark ward. At the end of the long corridor a door swings open emitting a bright shaft of light. Mina walks toward him. She is wearing a floor-length wedding dress, her face obscured behind a veil. Stopping at the side of his bed she takes Stephen by the hand. A voice, solemn as an undertaker's, comes over the hospital tannoy, intoning the words of a marriage ceremony. Stephen sits up as straight as he can and Mina stands beside him.

"I will."

"I will."

"I do."

"I do." When they say the vows their voices echo through the ward bouncing off the window beneath which flows the Thames.

Afterwards, Stephen woke. The large room was filled with a soft light although it was nowhere near dawn. Stephen turned his head: the man in the next bed was moaning with what sounded like pleasure. Beneath the hospital smells of chemicals and detergent Stephen thought he could smell something else, something more familiar, mud perhaps, perfume. Something had shifted Stephen felt, an adjustment had been made. It would all be all right in the end.

The night that Stephen came home was like a first night at the opera. He and Mina were both nervous. She took him to his flat in a taxi – she was carrying a large bag full of her own things. She intended to stay and take care of him.

Mina had missed Stephen while he was in hospital. She missed the presence of his body. She missed the things he had to say, the way she felt watched over by him. She was glad that he was all right. Life could continue now, steady like a pulse, like sleepy breathing. Mina felt satisfied. She could go back to work, trouble-free.

After dinner, Stephen sat in his armchair. He asked Mina to come out of the kitchen. He asked her to take off her clothes – he told her to get on top of him and fuck him immediately. Mina's cunt was tight and closed and firm; she forced herself down onto him and they both felt skin tear. She rocked back and forth, her eyes closed, her lips wet; Stephen grabbed hold of her breasts. Mina came very quickly, Stephen came shortly after her, gasping with pain. He called out her name.

Mina lifted herself off him then turned and sat in his lap. He held her in his arms, her head on his shoulder.

Later, she went into the bedroom. Stephen followed but sat down on the hard chair by his desk. "What are you doing?" Mina asked.

"I want to watch you sleeping," he said. "Go to sleep."

For a long time Stephen listened to Mina breathing. He turned in the chair to look out the window, pinching himself to stay awake. Thc moon was not out – the night was very dark.

Much later the room behind him seemed to lighten. He opened the window to let the night in, to let what was inside get out. And then, slowly, he turned around to look at what was there.

Mina is there. She is a vision. She is there for Stephen. A wind has come up in the room; Stephen lifts his head and breathes in the dark smell. He remembers what happened the night he ended up in the hospital. He remembers his dreams and his nightmares – now they have all come true. She is there before him, like love itself, an insubstantial shadow yet uncontrollable and daring. The room is full of light, fizzing, shifting. Stephen stares, dazzled as Mina comes near. Finally, she looks at herself, she must look at herself; his eyes are full of her reflection. They are both now close enough to see.